DOWN ON ME

J. KENNER

Down On Me

by

J. Kenner

Tight muscles. Vibrant Ink.
Meet Mr. January. Winter's never looked so hot ...

Certified bachelor Reece Walker wants two things—to save the local bar he manages and to get Jenna Montgomery into his bed.

He has a few ideas for the bar. But Jenna ... well, he's going to have to rely on cold showers, because she's been his best friend for years, and that's a line he just can't cross.

Until one wild kiss on a dark night changes everything. Now Reece is certain Jenna's meant to be his.

And with long nights in bed, sensual caresses, and deep, lingering kisses, he sets out to thoroughly convince her that friends can be lovers, too.

Down On Me is the first in a binge read series by New York Times, USA Today, Wall Street Journal, Publishers Weekly, and #1 International bestselling author of the million copy Stark series, J. Kenner.

Each book in the series is a STANDALONE novel with NO cliffhanger and a guaranteed HEA! But even so, you won't want to miss any in the series. Because then you can answer the question...

Who's Your Man of the Month?

Visit www.manofthemonthbooks.com to learn more!

Down on Me Copyright © 2018 by Julie Kenner

Cover design by Covers by Rogenna

Cover art by Perrywinkle Photography

ISBN: 978-1940673714

Published by Martini & Olive Books

v. 2018_1_10_P3

Chapter One

REECE WALKER RAN his palms over the slick, soapy ass of the woman in his arms and knew that he was going straight to hell.

Not because he'd slept with a woman he barely knew. Not because he'd enticed her into bed with a series of well-timed bourbons and particularly inventive half-truths. Not even because he'd lied to his best friend Brent about why Reece couldn't drive with him to the airport to pick up Jenna, the third player in their trifecta of lifelong friendship.

No, Reece was staring at the fiery pit because he was a lame, horny asshole without the balls to tell the naked beauty standing in the shower with him that she wasn't the woman he'd been thinking about for the last four hours.

And if that wasn't one of the pathways to hell, it damn sure ought to be.

He let out a sigh of frustration, and Megan tilted her head, one eyebrow rising in question as she slid her hand down to stroke his cock, which was demonstrating no guilt whatsoever about the whole going to hell issue. "Am I boring you?"

"Hardly." That, at least, was the truth. He felt like a prick, yes. But he was a well-satisfied one. "I was just thinking that you're beautiful."

She smiled, looking both shy and pleased—and Reece felt even more like a heel. What the devil was wrong with him? She *was* beautiful. And hot and funny and easy to talk to. Not to mention good in bed.

But she wasn't Jenna, which was a ridiculous comparison. Because Megan qualified as fair game, whereas Jenna was one of his two best friends. She trusted him. Loved him. And despite the way his cock perked up at the thought of doing all sorts of delicious things with her in bed, Reece knew damn well that would never happen. No way was he risking their friendship. Besides, Jenna didn't love him like that. Never had, never would.

And that—plus about a billion more reasons—meant that Jenna was entirely off-limits.

Too bad his vivid imagination hadn't yet gotten the memo.

Fuck it.

He tightened his grip, squeezing Megan's perfect rear. "Forget the shower," he murmured. "I'm taking you back to bed." He needed this. Wild. Hot. Demanding. And dirty enough to keep him from thinking.

Hell, he'd scorch the earth if that's what it took to burn Jenna from his mind—and he'd leave Megan limp, whimpering, and very, very satisfied. His guilt. Her pleasure. At least it would be a win for one of them.

And who knows? Maybe he'd manage to fuck the fantasies of his best friend right out of his head.

IT DIDN'T WORK.

Reece sprawled on his back, eyes closed, as Megan's gentle fingers traced the intricate outline of the tattoos inked across his pecs and down his arms. Her touch was warm and tender, in stark contrast to the way he'd just fucked her—a little too wild, a little too hard, as if he were fighting a battle, not making love.

Well, that was true, wasn't it?

But it was a battle he'd lost. Victory would have brought oblivion. Yet here he was, a naked woman beside him, and his thoughts still on Jenna, as wild and intense and impossible as they'd been since that night eight months ago when the earth had shifted beneath him, and he'd let himself look at her as a woman and not as a friend.

One breathtaking, transformative night, and Jenna didn't even realize it. And he'd be damned if he'd ever let her figure it out.

Beside him, Megan continued her exploration, one fingertip tracing the outline of a star. "No names? No wife or girlfriend's initials hidden in the design?"

He turned his head sharply, and she burst out laughing.

"Oh, don't look at me like that." She pulled the sheet up to cover her breasts as she rose to her knees beside him. "I'm just making conversation. No hidden agenda at all. Believe me, the last thing I'm interested in is a relationship." She scooted away, then sat on the edge of the bed, giving him an enticing view of her bare back. "I don't even do overnights."

As if to prove her point, she bent over, grabbed her bra off the floor, and started getting dressed.

"Then that's one more thing we have in common." He pushed himself up, rested his back against the headboard, and enjoyed the view as she wiggled into her jeans.

"Good," she said, with such force that he knew she

meant it, and for a moment he wondered what had soured her on relationships.

As for himself, he hadn't soured so much as fizzled. He'd had a few serious girlfriends over the years, but it never worked out. No matter how good it started, invariably the relationship crumbled. Eventually, he had to acknowledge that he simply wasn't relationship material. But that didn't mean he was a monk, the last eight months notwithstanding.

She put on her blouse and glanced around, then slipped her feet into her shoes. Taking the hint, he got up and pulled on his jeans and T-shirt. "Yes?" he asked, noticing the way she was eying him speculatively.

"The truth is, I was starting to think you might be in a relationship."

"What? Why?"

She shrugged. "You were so quiet there for a while, I wondered if maybe I'd misjudged you. I thought you might be married and feeling guilty."

Guilty.

The word rattled around in his head, and he groaned. "Yeah, you could say that."

"Oh, *hell*. Seriously?"

"No," he said hurriedly. "Not that. I'm not cheating on my non-existent wife. I wouldn't. Not ever." Not in small part because Reece wouldn't ever have a wife since he thought the institution of marriage was a crock, but he didn't see the need to explain that to Megan.

"But as for guilt?" he continued. "Yeah, tonight I've got that in spades."

She relaxed slightly. "Hmm. Well, sorry about the guilt, but I'm glad about the rest. I have rules, and I consider myself a good judge of character. It makes me cranky when I'm wrong."

"Wouldn't want to make you cranky."

"Oh, you really wouldn't. I can be a total bitch." She sat on the edge of the bed and watched as he tugged on his boots. "But if you're not hiding a wife in your attic, what are you feeling guilty about? I assure you, if it has anything to do with my satisfaction, you needn't feel guilty at all." She flashed a mischievous grin, and he couldn't help but smile back. He hadn't invited a woman into his bed for eight long months. At least he'd had the good fortune to pick one he actually liked.

"It's just that I'm a crappy friend," he admitted.

"I doubt that's true."

"Oh, it is," he assured her as he tucked his wallet into his back pocket. The irony, of course, was that as far as Jenna knew, he was an excellent friend. The best. One of her two pseudo-brothers with whom she'd sworn a blood oath the summer after sixth grade, almost twenty years ago.

From Jenna's perspective, Reece was at least as good as Brent, even if the latter scored bonus points because he was picking Jenna up at the airport while Reece was trying to fuck his personal demons into oblivion. Trying anything, in fact, that would exorcise the memory of how she'd clung to him that night, her curves enticing and her breath intoxicating, and not just because of the scent of too much alcohol.

She'd trusted him to be the white knight, her noble rescuer, and all he'd been able to think about was the feel of her body, soft and warm against his, as he carried her up the stairs to her apartment.

A wild craving had hit him that night, like a tidal wave of emotion crashing over him, washing away the outer shell of friendship and leaving nothing but raw desire and a longing so potent it nearly brought him to his knees.

It had taken all his strength to keep his distance when the only thing he'd wanted was to cover every inch of her naked body with kisses. To stroke her skin and watch her writhe with pleasure.

He'd won a hard-fought battle when he reined in his desire that night. But his victory wasn't without its wounds. She'd pierced his heart when she'd drifted to sleep in his arms, whispering that she loved him—and he knew that she meant it only as a friend.

More than that, he knew that he was the biggest asshole to ever walk the earth.

Thankfully, Jenna remembered nothing of that night. The liquor had stolen her memories, leaving her with a monster hangover, and him with a Jenna-shaped hole in his heart.

"Well?" Megan pressed. "Are you going to tell me? Or do I have to guess?"

"I blew off a friend."

"Yeah? That probably won't score you points in the Friend of the Year competition, but it doesn't sound too dire. Unless you were the best man and blew off the wedding? Left someone stranded at the side of the road somewhere in West Texas? Or promised to feed their cat and totally forgot? Oh, God. Please tell me you didn't kill Fluffy."

He bit back a laugh, feeling slightly better. "A friend came in tonight, and I feel like a complete shit for not meeting her plane."

"Well, there are taxis. And I assume she's an adult?"

"She is, and another friend is there to pick her up."

"I see," she said, and the way she slowly nodded suggested that she saw too much. "I'm guessing that *friend* means *girlfriend*? Or, no. You wouldn't do that. So she must be an ex."

"Really not," he assured her. "Just a friend. Lifelong, since sixth grade."

"Oh, I get it. Longtime friend. High expectations. She's going to be pissed."

"Nah. She's cool. Besides, she knows I usually work nights."

"Then what's the problem?"

He ran his hand over his shaved head, the bristles from the day's growth like sandpaper against his palm. "Hell if I know," he lied, then forced a smile, because whether his problem was guilt or lust or just plain stupidity, she hardly deserved to be on the receiving end of his bullshit.

He rattled his car keys. "How about I buy you one last drink before I take you home?"

"YOU'RE sure you don't mind a working drink?" Reece asked as he helped Megan out of his cherished baby blue vintage Chevy pickup. "Normally I wouldn't take you to my job, but we just hired a new bar back, and I want to see how it's going."

He'd snagged one of the coveted parking spots on Sixth Street, about a block down from The Fix, and he glanced automatically toward the bar, the glow from the windows relaxing him. He didn't own the place, but it was like a second home to him and had been for one hell of a long time.

"There's a new guy in training, and you're not there? I thought you told me you were the manager?"

"I did, and I am, but Tyree's there. The owner, I mean. He's always on site when someone new is starting. Says it's his job, not mine. Besides, Sunday's my day off, and Tyree's a stickler for keeping to the schedule."

"Okay, but why are you going then?"

"Honestly? The new guy's my cousin. He'll probably give me shit for checking in on him, but old habits die hard." Michael had been almost four when Vincent died, and the loss of his dad hit him hard. At sixteen, Reece had tried to be stoic, but Uncle Vincent had been like a second father to him, and he'd always thought of Mike as more brother than cousin. Either way, from that day on, he'd made it his job to watch out for the kid.

"Nah, he'll appreciate it," Megan said. "I've got a little sister, and she gripes when I check up on her, but it's all for show. She likes knowing I have her back. And as for getting a drink where you work, I don't mind at all."

As a general rule, late nights on Sunday were dead, both in the bar and on Sixth Street, the popular downtown Austin street that had been a focal point of the city's nightlife for decades. Tonight was no exception. At half-past one in the morning, the street was mostly deserted. Just a few cars moving slowly, their headlights shining toward the west, and a smattering of couples, stumbling and laughing. Probably tourists on their way back to one of the downtown hotels.

It was late April, though, and the spring weather was drawing both locals and tourists. Soon, the area—and the bar—would be bursting at the seams. Even on a slow Sunday night.

Situated just a few blocks down from Congress Avenue, the main downtown artery, The Fix on Sixth attracted a healthy mix of tourists and locals. The bar had existed in one form or another for decades, becoming a local staple, albeit one that had been falling deeper and deeper into disrepair until Tyree had bought the place six years ago and started it on much-needed life support.

"You've never been here before?" Reece asked as he

paused in front of the oak and glass doors etched with the bar's familiar logo.

"I only moved downtown last month. I was in Los Angeles before."

The words hit Reece with unexpected force. Jenna had been in LA, and a wave of both longing and regret crashed over him. He should have gone with Brent. What the hell kind of friend was he, punishing Jenna because he couldn't control his own damn libido?

With effort, he forced the thoughts back. He'd already beaten that horse to death.

"Come on," he said, sliding one arm around her shoulder and pulling open the door with his other. "You're going to love it."

He led her inside, breathing in the familiar mix of alcohol, southern cooking, and something indiscernible he liked to think of as the scent of a damn good time. As he expected, the place was mostly empty. There was no live music on Sunday nights, and at less than an hour to closing, there were only three customers in the front room.

"Megan, meet Cameron," Reece said, pulling out a stool for her as he nodded to the bartender in introduction. Down the bar, he saw Griffin Draper, a regular, lift his head, his face obscured by his hoodie, but his attention on Megan as she chatted with Cam about the house wines.

Reece nodded hello, but Griffin turned back to his notebook so smoothly and nonchalantly that Reece wondered if maybe he'd just been staring into space, thinking, and hadn't seen Reece or Megan at all. That was probably the case, actually. Griff wrote a popular podcast that had been turned into an even more popular web series, and when he wasn't recording the dialogue, he was usually writing a script.

"So where's Mike? With Tyree?"

Cameron made a face, looking younger than his twenty-four years. "Tyree's gone."

"You're kidding. Did something happen with Mike?" His cousin was a responsible kid. Surely he hadn't somehow screwed up his first day on the job.

"No, Mike's great." Cam slid a Scotch in front of Reece. "Sharp, quick, hard worker. He went off the clock about an hour ago, though. So you just missed him."

"Tyree shortened his shift?"

Cam shrugged. "Guess so. Was he supposed to be on until closing?"

"Yeah." Reece frowned. "He was. Tyree say why he cut him loose?"

"No, but don't sweat it. Your cousin's fitting right in. Probably just because it's Sunday and slow. " He made a face. "And since Tyree followed him out, guess who's closing for the first time alone."

"So you're in the hot seat, huh? " Reece tried to sound casual. He was standing behind Megan's stool, but now he moved to lean against the bar, hoping his casual posture suggested that he wasn't worried at all. He was, but he didn't want Cam to realize it. Tyree didn't leave employees to close on their own. Not until he'd spent weeks training them.

"I told him I want the weekend assistant manager position. I'm guessing this is his way of seeing how I work under pressure."

"Probably," Reece agreed half-heartedly. "What did he say?"

"Honestly, not much. He took a call in the office, told Mike he could head home, then about fifteen minutes later said he needed to take off, too, and that I was the man for the night."

"Trouble?" Megan asked.

"No. Just chatting up my boy," Reece said, surprised at how casual his voice sounded. Because the scenario had trouble printed all over it. He just wasn't sure what kind of trouble.

He focused again on Cam. "What about the waitstaff?" Normally, Tiffany would be in the main bar taking care of the customers who sat at tables. "He didn't send them home, too, did he?"

"Oh, no," Cam said. "Tiffany and Aly are scheduled to be on until closing, and they're in the back with—"

But his last words were drowned out by a high-pitched squeal of "*You're here!*" and Reece looked up to find Jenna Montgomery—the woman he craved—barreling across the room and flinging herself into his arms.

Chapter Two

"I DIDN'T THINK I'd see you until tomorrow." Excitement laced Jenna's voice, and she clung to him with gleeful ferocity. Her arms tightened around his neck, and her legs—strong from years of cycling the Austin hills—captured his waist with a vise-grip. "What a fabulous surprise!"

When she'd launched herself at him—her long, ginger hair flying behind her—he'd stumbled backward from the force of her enthusiasm, locking his arms around her in reflex. Now he continued to hold her tight, relishing this delicious, stolen moment with her curves pressed soft against him and her heartbeat reverberating through him. She was close enough that he could count her freckles, and her breath was intoxicating, smelling of lime and Corona and rum. Just like it had that night.

"Loaded Coronas," he murmured, his body tightening with the memory of that other time when he'd held her close and breathed that heady scent.

"Cam made me one." She loosened her grip, and all he had to do was let go so that she could slip out of his arms. It should have been easy. Instead, it felt as though he were holding a live wire, sparking all the wild and heated impulses he'd worked so hard to suppress.

She started to squirm, obviously intending to slide down his body, basically using him like a stripper pole. Not that Jenna would think of it that way. To her, she was just getting back on her feet. But in the process, she'd undoubtedly feel the evidence of the dangerous direction his mind was wandering.

That, he thought, would be a very bad thing.

So, with a heroic effort, he closed his hands around her waist and eased her to the ground, keeping enough distance between them that there was no contact between her body and his crotch.

"In fact," she continued, as if there'd been no gap at all in the conversation, "I think Cam needs to make me another." She winked at Reece, her green eyes twinkling. "They really are amazing."

"Amazing," he repeated, his eyes narrowing with both amusement and mock reprobation. "I seem to remember you telling me they were sneaky, dangerous drinks, and that I was an evil genius for thinking them up in the first place."

One shoulder lifted in a casual shrug as she headed toward the bar where Cameron was pouring the neck off of a fresh Corona before filling the space with rum. She wore her shoulder-length hair parted in the middle, and it fell like sheets of fire around her shoulders. "They are, and you are, and they're still damn delicious," Jenna announced. "Besides, my flight was horrible. I deserve this." She took the finished drink from Cam, pulled a long swallow, and made the kind of satisfied noise a man likes to hear from a woman in bed.

Reece shifted again, trying to dissuade his cock from leaping to attention, then felt a wash of metaphorical cold water splash over him when Megan came up beside him, her eyes dancing with amusement. "I'm guessing this is the friend who flew in tonight?"

"This is indeed," Jenna said, thrusting her hand out to Megan. "I'm Jenna. And I'm guessing you're the reason my so-called best friend blew me off?"

From down the bar, Reece heard Griff stifle a laugh. He rolled his eyes and scowled at Jenna. "Come on, Jen. You know I—"

But Jenna held up her hand, cutting him off. "I'm teasing. Brent's perfectly capable of picking me up. And it looks like you had other plans, anyway," she added, eyeing Megan with what appeared to be approval before taking another long sip.

His gut tightened. He wanted to tell her that Megan was a great girl, but she wasn't *his* girl. Right then, that seemed to be the most important thing in the world.

Fortunately, he recognized the asinine impulse for what it was, and shifted the topic entirely. "Speaking of Brent, where is he?"

Jenna started to turn, probably to find Brent and call him over. But before she answered, Megan gasped.

"Jenna?" Her voice rose with incredulity. "Oh my gosh, I thought you looked familiar. You organized the Kempinski wedding, right?"

For a moment, Jenna looked baffled, then her eyes widened. "Makeup Megan! What on earth are you doing in Austin? For that matter, why are you slumming with that one?" She hooked her thumb toward Reece, her voice teasing.

"Makeup Megan?" Reece repeated. "What the hell?"

"She's a makeup artist." Jenna looked from Megan to Reece. "Didn't you know?"

Megan's lips twitched as she took Reece's hand. "Let's just say that we're still getting to know each other."

Jenna's brows rose as she faced Reece. She looked amused. Reece wasn't sharing the emotion. "We met in LA," she said. "Megan did some work for my first and only event for the evil Company That Shall Not Be Named," Jenna explained, then finished off her drink.

"Oh, you got caught up in that crap?" Megan asked. "I'm so sorry."

Cam had slid out from under the bar to settle the check of the two customers sitting at a table. Now they were walking out the door, and he was splitting the cash they'd left on the table between the till and the tip jar. "What crap?" he asked, after raising a hand and telling them to have a good night. "What happened?"

"A long, sad story," Jenna said, climbing up onto a stool. She pushed the empty Corona bottle toward Cam. "I think we need another round of these before I dredge it all up. And before we all turn into pumpkins at closing."

Cam looked to Reece, who shrugged. "So long as she's buying and not driving, I won't say no to a customer. As to the long, sad story, though..."

Jenna shrugged. "Okay, fine. It's not that long. Asshole company lured me to LA with promises of great opportunities. They went bankrupt. I couldn't find another decent job since I don't have the experience I expected to get from the Evil Bastards Who Must Be Cursed. Then my landlord tells me I have to move because he's selling the building. And to top it off, my car dies, and it would cost more to fix it than I happen to have in my meager little bank account." She made a face. "So I sold it for basically nothing, used the money for a plane ticket, then turned tail and ran—or, rather, *flew*—home to my friends and family. End of sob story." She tilted her head to look at Megan. "What about you? How'd you end up in Austin?"

"My story's neither long nor interesting," she said. "I fell for the wrong guy. Boom. The end."

"Not this guy, I hope." Jenna narrowed her eyes at Reece. "'Cause I can smack him down if you need me to."

"I don't know him well enough yet to identify his faults," Megan said, and from down the bar, Reece heard Griff laugh again. "But what I need to know right now is what's in these things?" She snatched up one of the Loaded Coronas that Cam had lined up on the bar.

"Try it," Reece urged, grateful she'd derailed the direction of the conversation. Jenna tended to play matchmaker, and Reece and Brent were her favorite victims. Before, it hadn't bothered him. Now, he couldn't stand the thought of Jenna pushing him toward anyone.

"They're my own invention," he told Megan, grabbing a bottle for himself before settling down on one of the barstools. "And they've become a favorite on the bar menu. You want one, Griff?" he called down to the end of the bar. "On the house."

"No thanks," Griff said, turning his head just a bit, but keeping his face in shadows. "I'm good."

Reece almost argued. He happened to know that Griff loved the things. Which meant he'd already had too much of something else to drink, or he didn't want Megan to see the scars that marred the right side of his face and body. Considering Griff habitually had only one bourbon and then a steady stream of club soda when he came to the bar to work, Reece's money was on the latter.

Griff had moved to Austin almost two years ago, and he and Reece had hit it off. The circle of friends had quickly widened to include Brent and Jenna and Tyree. Now, most everyone who worked at The Fix knew about his scars and didn't blink. But that didn't extend to strangers, and although Reece was confident Megan wouldn't flinch, he wasn't inclined to force Griff out of his comfort zone.

"They're dangerous," Jenna was telling Megan when Reece tuned back into the conversation. "Pace yourself."

"Rum, Corona, salted lime," Reece retorted. "What's dangerous about that?"

"They're too tasty. As you damn well know." She settled back on her stool, rotating it until she was facing him. Then she casually lifted one foot and propped it up on the seat of his barstool—which placed it right between his legs. She wore wedge-style sandals that showed off her polished toenails, and he had to call on every ounce of mental fortitude to concentrate on what she was saying and ignore the fantasies about what she could do with those wildly sexy feet.

"I got wasted on these things," she continued. "It was the night before I moved to LA, and I was so nervous I kept slamming them back, and then—" She cut herself off with a shrug.

"And then what?" Cam asked, leaning forward.

"Beats me. I passed completely out." Jenna smiled and batted her eyes. "He swears he didn't take advantage of me, but you never know..."

"For Christ's sake, Jenna," Reece snapped. "Why the hell would you even say—"

"Sorry, sorry!" She held up her hands in apology, then aimed a thin smile at Megan. "I was teasing. Reece would never do anything like that. Certainly not with me—I mean, he thinks of me like a sister—but not with anyone, either. He's one of the good ones."

"I believe you," Megan said, her tender expression reminding him of why taking her home tonight seemed like a good idea.

He gently pushed Jenna's foot down, then stood up. "I

think it's time to get back on track. Cam, Tyree took you through the closing procedure, right?"

"Um, not really. I told you. He just kind of left."

Reece's concern, which had begun to dwindle during the banter with Jenna and Megan, ramped up again. "You're telling me that Tyree—the owner of this bar and the only manager on the premises then—just walked out, leaving a bartender who's never closed before without any instructions on what to do?"

Cam hunched his shoulders, looking younger than his twenty-four years. "Um, pretty much."

Reece told himself to stay chill. This wasn't a crisis yet. "Where did you say Aly and Tiffany were?" he asked, referring to two of the wait staff.

"They're in the back doing prep," Jenna said. "I was talking with them when I heard you come in."

"Brent's back there, too?" Reece couldn't believe he hadn't asked earlier. But he'd been so thrilled to see Jenna —and so concerned about Tyree—that he hadn't wondered where the hell Brent had got off to.

"Brent went into the office to check on something right after he and Jen got here," Cam said as he started to wipe down the bar. He looked calmer now that he had a solid answer to a question. "Then about half an hour ago he rushed out. Didn't say where he was going. Just that he had to check on something, but..." He trailed off with a shrug. "Jenna says he's her ride, so I figure he'll be back soon. He knows we're closing."

The alarm bells that had been softly tolling in Reece's head started to clang. First Tyree, then Brent. And considering Brent was in charge of the bar's security, if he was seeing trouble, then Reece felt justified in worrying.

Not that he could do anything about it at the moment. Best to just slide into his job and make sure everything outstanding was taken care off. "Right, then. Cam, you go ahead and start going through your usual end-of-shift checklist. Griffin, are you heading out, or are you going to stay and finish up?"

Griff tapped his notebook with his pen. "Just a little longer if that's okay, then I'll get out of your hair."

"No rush," Reece assured him, then turned to Jenna. "Will you go let Aly and Tiffany know that I'll be back. But they should finish up their prep, let Cam know when they're done, then clock out. If I'm not back, I'll see them both on their next shift."

"Sure, but what do you mean back? Where are you going?"

"I'm going to take Megan home. Sorry tonight turned crazy," he continued, shifting his attention to Megan. "I only thought we'd grab a drink and check in on my cousin. I didn't expect ... well, any of this."

"Not a problem." She leaned forward and kissed his cheek. "Really."

He swallowed, then noticed Jenna watching him. Not with her usual effervescent expression. Now she seemed pensive—and he couldn't help but wonder what question she was trying to work out.

"Right." He cleared his throat. "Back in a bit," he said to Cam and Jenna. "Ready?" he added, turning to Megan.

"Sure, but I live at the Railyard," she said, referring to a condominium complex just a few blocks over on Fourth Street. "If you need to work, I can get there on my own."

"At two in the morning? Screw that. I'll drive you."

He thought she might argue, but all she did was offer him her arm. They'd just taken a step toward the exit when the door flew open, and Brent burst inside, his expression tight, his hands clenched, and his brown eyes blazing with restrained fury.

"What's the matt—" Reece began, but Brent cut him off with a curt, "We need to talk."

"I'll just walk home," Megan said, pulling her arm free and smiling gently. "Honestly, I'll be fine. I do it all the time."

"No." Reece held up a finger, signaling Brent to wait for one second as he focused on Megan. "Why don't you—"

"I'll see her home," Griff said firmly. He stood up and crossed to Megan, close enough so that she couldn't miss the scars hidden in the shadow of his hood. "My car's parked over by the Railyard, and it's time for me to get going anyway." He lifted one shoulder in a casual shrug. "Assuming that's okay with you?"

"Yeah, fine by me," she said, without the slightest hesitation. She glanced at Reece. "He's your friend, right? Because my mother warned me against talking to strangers."

"Griffin Draper," Griff said. "And yeah, Reece claims me." He thrust out his right hand, also covered with scars, and Reece couldn't help but think he was testing her. Since she shook it, he assumed that she'd passed.

"Thanks, Griff." Reece patted his friend on the back. "Appreciate it."

"Tonight was fun," Megan said to Reece, rising up on her tiptoes to brush a kiss across his cheek. "We'll have another drink soon?"

"Hell, yeah," he said, forcing himself not to look at Jenna. And at the same time reminding himself that this was good. This was what he needed. A woman in his life for a little fun, a little sex. A woman who was good in bed and easy-going in the world.

A woman who held no expectations and had no agenda and no interest in getting involved.

Most important, a woman who wasn't Jenna.

"Cam, lock the door and finish up," Brent ordered, the moment they disappeared around the corner. He pointed to Reece. "And you meet me in the office. We need to talk."

"This is about Tyree, I assume?" Reece said, as soon as Jenna shut the door behind them. Brent hadn't invited her specifically, but they'd fallen back into old habits, and the three of them were a team. "What the hell's going on?"

"Is it Elijah?" Jenna asked, referring to Tyree's sixteen-year-old son. His mom—Tyree's wife—had been killed in a car wreck seven years before, and they'd both had a hard time of it for a while. But as far as Reece knew, they were both doing better, and Eli was thriving in school.

Brent pinched the bridge of his nose. "It's the bar," he said, his voice heavy with emotion. "He's on the verge of losing this entire damn place."

Chapter Three

"WHAT THE HELL?" Jenna lowered herself into one of the two guest chairs, because her knees had just been knocked out from under her. "Losing The Fix? How is that even possible?"

Beside her, Reece ran his hand over his shaved head, his mouth curving down into a frown. He'd decided to shave his thick black hair right before she'd moved from Austin to LA eight months ago. In fact, one of the last things Jenna remembered from the drunken night before she'd left for LA was rubbing her hand over his scalp, then telling him she had to kiss it for luck.

To him, she was sure, the caress was innocent.

To her, it delved into decadent fantasies about what might happen if he tilted his face up so that her kiss fell on his lips instead of his head. And her imagination had generated some *serious* heat.

Not that she'd ever get close enough to that fire to truly feel the burn. That was a fire that had to stay locked away tight in the realm of fantasy.

Reece and Brent were her best friends, after all. Her

pillars, her anchors. And there was no way she'd ever, *ever*, do something to screw that up. She never even thought about Reece like that.

Except apparently, she did. Especially after *that* night.

The night before she'd left for LA, when they'd gone out drinking and dancing with friends, with extra emphasis on the drinking part. Brent had to bow out because of a minor crisis, and Reece had taken her home, then carried her up the stairs to her apartment since she'd been too far gone to manage on her own.

He'd held her—taken care of her—and when she'd fallen headlong into sleep, the little demons that lived in the liquor had plucked hidden strands of lust from her innocent thoughts, then weaved them into a tapestry of prurient decadence that had infiltrated her dreams, leaving her to wake up the following morning needy, frustrated, and more than a little embarrassed.

That was eight long months ago. Even so, she felt her cheeks burn with the memory right now. She squirmed in Tyree's guest chair, crossing and uncrossing her legs, the inopportune memory teasing her. In the process, she glanced sideways—and was brought up short when she saw Reece frowning at her as if she was a puzzle. Or worse, as if he could see right through her pink cheeks and into her lust-red thoughts.

"I'm not—" She cut herself off, unsure what she'd planned to say. It didn't matter. He didn't even hear her, and she realized that his expression was because of Tyree's predicament and not because her cheeks were flaming under her freckles.

Duh.

"Is it foreclosure?" Reece aimed the question at Brent, then leaned against the battered bookshelf, his arms crossed over his chest. "I know receipts are down—the competition downtown has gotten crazy—but I didn't think it was so bad that he couldn't make the mortgage."

"It shouldn't be," Brent said. "But apparently he's got until the end of the year to pay off the mortgage in full—and that can't be a small chunk of change. If he can't manage, it's *adios* to all of this."

"That's crazy." Jenna looked from one guy to the other. "Are you sure?"

"I came in here to reboot the security cameras, and I accidentally bumped his mouse." An ex-cop, Brent was in charge of all aspects of security at the bar. Everything from escorting out rowdy patrons to examining questionable IDs to checking employee references. And, of course, he ensured that the video security was always up and running. "The demand letter was on the screen. I shouldn't have read it, but..."

"The hell you shouldn't," Jenna said. "How else would we know he needs help?" She twisted in her seat, positioning herself to make eye contact with both guys. "We are helping, right?"

"Hell, yeah," they said in unison, making her smile. "The question is how," Reece added.

"And why he needs help in the first place," Brent added.

Reece took a step toward him. "Show me the letter. Maybe there's something relevant in the text that you missed."

"Can't," Brent said, lowering himself into Tyree's desk chair with a sigh. "The hard drive went to sleep when I went out to meet you two, and now I can't log in without his password. No idea why it wasn't locked down before, but we all know this computer is a piece of shit."

Jenna bit back a laugh. That was true. She'd waited tables for The Fix when she was finishing grad school, and

Tyree used to let her work on class papers during her breaks. The computer was an ancient beast, but he refused to replace it, always saying that any spare cash needed to either go into the bar or toward Elijah's college fund. So long as the computer was computing, then he didn't need some fancy upgrade.

"Maybe he got behind on his payments?" Reece suggested, but Jenna heard the incredulity in his voice, and she agreed with it. She didn't know Tyree as well as Reece or Brent did, but she was certain that the efficient ex-military officer wouldn't let that happen.

"Well, something's up," Brent said. "But honestly, it's getting on toward three, and I've got a babysitter to pay." He rose, then scrubbed a hand over his jaw and close-trimmed beard. "Why don't we talk over breakfast tomorrow? I'll drop Faith at kindergarten, go for a jog, and be back by nine, easy."

Reece nodded. "Sounds good. I'm going to hang here for a bit—make sure everything's set for the morning."

Brent clapped him on the shoulder. "The sacred duty of the bar manager." He pointed a finger at Reece. "Don't forget to set the alarm. And you," he added, gesturing for Jenna to follow, "are with me."

"Right," she said, rising and moving toward the door. Reece was doing the same, and they caused a minor logjam. She shifted, brushing against him, then shivered from the unexpected shock of electricity that rushed through her from nothing more than that innocent contact.

"You okay?" Reece put his hand on her shoulder, and when she looked up, she thought for a moment that she'd get lost inside the smoky quartz of his eyes. "Jenna?"

"Huh?" She blinked. "Oh, yeah. I'm just—you know. I'm not used to bar hours. And with the flying and getting up early and the travel and the drinking—"

"Dead on your feet," he said. "Get some sleep, and I'll see you tomorrow."

"Sure." He started to pull her in for a hug, the same way he'd done a million times over the years, but he stopped short and straightened, then stretched as if he'd been overcome with exhaustion.

Something in the back of her mind told her she should be confused. Or maybe even annoyed. Possibly worried. Because something was off-kilter, for sure.

Instead, all she felt was relief.

"Tomorrow," she said, firmly, then followed Reece out the door.

"THANKS FOR LETTING ME CRASH HERE," Jenna said, flopping onto the familiar, tattered couch the moment the babysitter was out the door. "Amanda said I could sleep in her living room, but honestly, the idea of sleeping there while her parents are in the house..." She trailed off with a shake of her head. "I love them, but that's a little too close for comfort."

Amanda Franklin and Jenna had shared a dorm for three of their four undergraduate years at the University of Texas, and Amanda was by far Jenna's closest girlfriend. Also an Austin local, Amanda had frequently visited her parents' lakeside house for meals, laundry, and effusive hugs. She'd dragged Jenna along, and once the Franklins learned that Jenna had no family other than a single mom who worked too many hours for too little money, they'd adopted both of the Montgomery women into the fold.

The plan had been for Jenna to crash with Amanda until she got a new job and a place of her own. Amanda was off work for the week, and they were going to spend the next couple of nights drinking and watching bawdy girl movies and eating raw cookie dough.

The plan, however, was no more. Amanda's parents had found themselves homeless while their flooring was being replaced after an unanticipated water heater disaster. Instead of a hotel, they'd moved in with Amanda.

Jenna loved Martha and Huey Franklin dearly, but that didn't mean she wanted to be front and center in the living room where they could ask her question after question about why the job in LA didn't work out (she'd been caught in the crossfire of really bad management) or what she intended to do now (she had no idea, and the thought of her dwindling bank account was making her queasy).

Better to stay with Brent and visit the Franklins when she'd had sleep and pre-rehearsed responses to all of their well-meaning, but gut-twisting questions.

"Tell you what," Brent said. "*I'll* sleep in the living room, and you take my bed."

Jenna wanted to kick her own ass. "No, no. I didn't mean it like that. You know I didn't."

He brushed the words away, then went down the short hallway and into the kitchen. The small house in Austin's Crestview neighborhood was old enough not to have an open floor plan. She couldn't see him anymore, but from where she sat in the cozy living room she could hear him opening and closing cabinets.

"Dammit, Brent. I'm not kicking you out of your bed. *Your* living room is fine."

"I'm not talking forever," Brent clarified, his low voice carrying easily to her. "Just tonight. You take my bed. Tomorrow, Faith can start sleeping with me. I'd move her tonight, but she'd never get back to sleep."

Jenna pushed herself off the couch and went into the

kitchen, taking a seat at the small breakfast table by the window. "I'm not kicking your little girl out of her bed."

"My house, my rules." He grinned, revealing the dimple in his left cheek. "Here," he added, sliding a cup of hot chocolate in front of her and then taking the seat across from her. "You're exhausted, and you know it. You'll sleep better in the bed. And I can sleep anywhere."

"Fine." She wasn't conceding, but the battle was going to have to wait, because the adrenaline rush that had accompanied the news of Tyree's money problems was fading, leaving her too wiped out to argue. "You don't look tired at all."

He shrugged. "When you combine single dad with working bar hours, you end up with a guy who's at his best at weird times of the day."

"Maybe you're secretly Superman," she teased, then hid her grin in the whipped cream that topped her cocoa. Still, it wasn't a bad comparison. He even had a Clark Kent thing going lately. A Nice Single Dad Next Door persona that mostly eclipsed his panty-dropping good looks.

But that was only the image he showed the world now. Jenna had known him for most of her life. Before he was a cop. Before that bitch Olivia.

Jenna had seen him in swim trunks at the beach during college, his skin glowing with a tan, his body so tight and strong that Jenna was certain all the other girls on the beach had whiplash.

During that same trip, she'd seen Brent and Reece stand up for a confused homeless man against a gang of dangerous-looking locals. The three of them had gone to Corpus for a weekend one summer and had stumbled across a klatch of thugs giving the guy shit, stealing food from the grocery cart that doubled as his home, and making a point of kicking sand at him whenever they passed by.

Brent had led the charge, but Reece had been right beside him. Her guys had shut that shit down with no-nonsense language and a couple of well-placed punches. It was the first time she'd seen them fight together since elementary school, and the depth of their friendship had been reflected in the way they anticipated each other, covered each other. They were so different. Reece, ripped, tattooed and bearded even back then. Brent, all lean muscle, strength, and speed.

She drew in a breath, then sighed with the memory. They were both such great guys, not to mention ridiculously good looking.

But it's Reece you want.

The voice in her head startled her, and she jerked her mug, getting whipped cream all over her upper lip.

"You okay?" Brent put his hand on her shoulder, and she waited for her body to react the same way it had when she'd brushed up against Reece earlier. Because maybe it had just been a reflex. A little bit of sizzle, normal for a girl who hadn't been with a guy in ages.

Except she wasn't reacting now. No zing. No buzz. No heated flurries or spinning butterflies. Just her and Brent and the reassuring pressure on her shoulder.

Nothing like she'd felt with Reece.

So what the hell did that mean?

"Hey?" He squeezed her shoulder. "You in there?"

"Sorry. I'm just—I don't know," she ended lamely because she was hardly going to tell him that her mind had wandered to their mutual best friend.

"You're fading fast," Brent said, a chuckle in his voice.

"I need sleep. But can I see Faith first? If you don't think we'll wake her?"

A tender smile touched Brent's lips, and she felt her heart squeeze. He'd sacrificed so much for that little girl, and never even thought twice about it.

She rinsed her mug, then put it in the drainer before following him to the smaller of the two bedrooms in the house. He turned the knob slowly, then pushed the door partway open.

A pink night-light cast just enough glow for Jenna to see the little girl sprawled on her back, her sheet and blanket having been kicked off. She hugged a stuffed tiger with one arm, and the other thumb was in her mouth. Jenna could hear the sucking noise from where they stood and felt tears prick her eyes. It was good to be back in Austin with her friends.

"I can't believe she's already five," Jenna said once Brent had closed the door. "I feel like I missed years."

"She's growing fast." Pride laced his voice. He hesitated, then looked her in the eyes. "And even though I'm sorry about your job, I'm glad you're back."

"I was just thinking that," she admitted as they headed into the bedroom. "I'm nervous about money—the job market's crappy. But I'm glad I'm back, too."

"You'll be fine," he said, easing his arm around her. She leaned against him, and it was comfortable. Easy. Nothing at all like it would be if she were leaning against Reece.

If that were the case, her pulse would be pounding like crazy, and her entire body would have so much energy coursing through it that she could personally light up all of Central Texas.

Clearing her throat, she took what she hoped was a casual step back. If Brent noticed anything off, he didn't comment. Instead, he opened the dresser drawer, took out a pair of pajama bottoms and a plain T-shirt, then headed for the bathroom. "Back in a sec," he said, shutting the door behind him.

She perched on the edge of the bed, exhaustion warring with restlessness. "What do you think of Megan?" she called after a moment.

"Who?"

Unexpected relief swept over her; if Brent didn't know who Megan was, that meant it wasn't serious between her and Reece.

"Megan," she repeated. "I knew her in LA. I think maybe she's dating Reece."

"Yeah?" He stepped out of the bathroom, now in PJs. "Let me scrounge up a blanket, and then I'll bring your suitcase in here for you."

"You didn't know? Must not be that serious."

He bent to open a wooden trunk, but glanced up, his brow furrowed. "Don't you like her?"

"What? Of course I like her," she said quickly, wondering what exactly her tone of voice had revealed. Because she *did* like Megan. She just didn't want her dating Reece. Which was stupid, because she wanted both Reece and Brent to be happy. With wives and families and picket fences.

"About time, if you ask me," Brent said, interrupting her thoughts.

"What do you mean?

He stood, a bundle of blankets and sheets in his arms. "Well, you know our guy. Date, get serious, break up. As regular as the phases of the moon. Or it was. He hasn't dated in months. Not even hookups, as far as I know." He headed out the door, his voice coming back from the living room. "But now there's a new woman. Even better, she's one you can vouch for. I'd say it's a good sign. Don't you?"

he added, returning with her suitcase and plunking it down by the foot of the bed.

"Yeah. Of course." She cleared her throat, hating how weak her voice sounded. "Speaking of, who have you been seeing?"

"Ah, that would be the stunning Miss Not Yet In The Picture." He spoke in a fake British accent, and she laughed, knowing that he was referencing—badly—*Monty Python and the Holy Grail*, one of the movies the three of them had watched as kids, convinced they were watching something risqué and wildly inappropriate.

"You should date more. Find someone. Faith needs—"

"Don't tell me Faith needs a mom." There was steel in his voice. "Faith has a mom. She definitely doesn't need two of that breed."

"Don't lump all women in with Olivia," Jenna said, wishing she'd kept her mouth shut.

For a second, she thought he was going to ignore her. Then he drew a breath and shook his head. "No," he said with a soft smile. "I wouldn't dream of it." He reached out and gently stroked her cheek. "Maybe we should just run off to Vegas. You'd be a great mom."

"You better believe I would," she retorted. "I'm good in bed, too."

"Well, we have that in common," he countered, making her laugh. She knew he wasn't even remotely serious—and she wasn't even remotely tempted—so there was no weirdness twisting in her gut.

"Of course, that would be breaking our oath," he teased.

She made a B in sign language with her fingers and put it up on her forehead, the supposedly secret sign they'd come up with the summer she'd turned eleven. "Best friends forever, right? The Three Musketeers."

"Or three blind mice, depending on your point of view. But yeah. An oath is an oath."

"Hell yeah," she said softy. She looked at Brent, but her mind was on a different guy.

"And call me crazy, but I want to marry for love. And sex. But mostly love."

She pressed a hand to her heart in mock indignation. "Are you saying you don't love me?"

"I love you to the moon and back. But not like that."

"I know." She drew in a breath, then yawned. "Me, too."

"You're exhausted." He kissed her forehead. "Now go to sleep. It's past three, and Reece will be here early."

He headed out then, shutting the door behind him, and Jenna was left staring around the room, which was illuminated by the faint glow of a streetlight seeping in around the curtains. She wanted to curl up in bed and crash. Half an hour ago, she would have. Hell, even five minutes ago. She'd been tired, then. Completely drained.

And then Brent had gone and mentioned Reece, and now her body was purring, forbidden memories sliding up to tease her senses.

And then he'd mentioned friendship and oaths, and she wished she could pry all those decadent, unwanted thoughts and feelings from her mind.

She opened her suitcase and started to unpack. She pulled out her make-up case and took all of her cosmetics into the bathroom, then laid them out for the morning. She hoped the familiar travel routine would distract her.

It didn't. Reece was still in her mind. Heated thoughts. Sensual meanderings. And maybe she shouldn't try to shut it off. Maybe she should just go with it.

Back in the bedroom, she got undressed, slipped into a nightshirt, then climbed into bed. Because she'd decided to give in to temptation. To close her eyes and remember a night when she'd gotten way too drunk.

A night when Reece had taken care of her, then carried her to bed.

A night he thought she didn't remember.

But she did. Some of it, at least.

And as a warm blush spread over her body, Jenna closed her eyes, breathed deep, and let herself fall backward into the memories of that delicious, forbidden night.

Chapter Four

Eight months ago

"YOU AND BRENT should just quit working and move to LA with me." Jenna took another long swallow of the rum and Corona concoction, then sighed with pleasure, her head spinning a little more than it should. Correction, a *lot* more than it should. "These are amazing. You're putting them on the menu, right?"

"If you say so, I will. Your wish is my command."

"You're teasing me, aren't you?" She narrowed her eyes, saw two of him, then narrowed them some more until Reece merged into one man. A man who was smiling indulgently at her from across one of the wooden two-tops in the back section of The Fix on Sixth.

Seven Percent, a local band that had gathered a nation-wide following, was playing on the wooden stage up front, and normally she'd be sitting at the bar up there, listening to the music and chatting with the bartenders or a girl-friend while Brent and Reece did their jobs. Tonight, however, they'd both taken the night off. Because tonight was Zero Hour. The last hurrah.

Tomorrow at noon she was getting into her car and driving to Los Angeles.

"Where'd Brent go? He's not off doing work on my last day in town, is he?" She swiveled in her chair to search for her errant friend, tilted awkwardly, and then smiled gratefully when Reece reached over to steady her.

"You're drunk," he said. Not in accusation, but as one might state the weather.

"It's your fault." She lifted the beer bottle. "Your invention. Your fault. And I do say. In honor of me."

"You do say?" he repeated, rubbing his beard as his brow furrowed in confusion before clearing. "Oh, about the drink going on the menu. All right. In honor of you. I'll call them Long Neck Jennas."

She wrinkled her nose. "That's horrible."

"Got a better name?"

She squinted at the longneck bottle. Rum. Corona. Lime. One bottle, all loaded up. She smiled up at him. "Loaded Coronas."

His mouth twitched. He reached across the table, then brushed his fingertip over the tip of her nose. "Done."

"Yeah?"

"Assuming Tyree agrees."

"Let's ask him."

"He's with Brent, remember?"

She shook her head to clear it, trying to play back the last half hour or so.

Watching her, Reece laughed. "You are *so* wasted."

"So? Last hurrah, remember? Besides, it dulls the pain."

He took her hands. "Hey, none of that. This is a good

thing, remember? Just one month ago, you told me so yourself."

The memory of the phone call offering her the job in Los Angeles set off a fresh storm of emotion. "You're right. It is. I mean, the company's got an amazing reputation, and I'm going to get so much experience. It's a dream job —working with a premier event planner in Beverly Hills. It's exactly the kind of job I was hoping for when I quit teaching to go back for my marketing degree. I mean, a company that's behind most celebrity charity events? Half of my graduating class would kill for this job."

"But?"

She raised a shoulder. "Just nerves, I guess. I'm almost twenty-nine, and I've never lived anywhere but Austin. And, well, I'll miss you guys."

A shadow flickered in his eyes. "Yeah, I know. We'll miss you, too. But it's not forever. You get the experience, you move back to Texas, and you take the city by storm."

Laughter bubbled up in her. "Is that the plan?"

"Written in stone, baby. I've got all sorts of faith in you."

"I know you do," she said softly, meaning the words with all her heart. "And it helps."

For a moment, a pleasant silence lingered. Then she tilted her head toward the hall leading to the office. "Should we go find Brent? We're supposed to meet Amanda at the Broken Spoke." Jenna was lousy at country-western dancing, but there was no way she was leaving Texas without another go. And besides, Brent could two-step like a pro. If anyone could make her look good on a dance floor, it was him.

"Probably should. But you've had four of those things, and that's a lot of rum. Not to mention the beer. Are you sure you can dance?"

"Oh, please. We both know I couldn't dance before. There's no place to go but up." Laughing, she slid an arm around his waist, for both camaraderie and support. He stiffened, then relaxed, and she was about to ask what was wrong when Brent came toward them, his expression grave.

"What is it?" Reece demanded.

"My babysitter called. Faith has a fever. I'm sorry, Jen, but I need to go."

"Sure. Of course. We'll come with you."

"No, you guys go on. This is your last chance to see Amanda before you head out, right? She can't do breakfast tomorrow?"

Jenna nodded. They were supposed to meet up at the Magnolia Cafe on South Congress before Jenna hit the road. "But if Faith's sick, I won't see you tomorrow either."

"I'll make pancakes. Come to the house. I already told Tyree, and I'll text Nolan and Tiffany and everyone else. I can set Faith up in my bedroom with her videos if she's still sick, and we'll give you a banana pancake send-off."

"You sure?"

"Are you kidding? Not see you off? Not a chance. Ten o'clock?"

She nodded. The plan was to be on the road by noon, stay the night in Van Horn, the next night in Phoenix, then get to her new—sight unseen—apartment by mid-afternoon. She had a thermos for coffee, an ice chest for sandwiches, and a ton of playlists downloaded to her phone. She was as ready as she'd ever be, but no way was she leaving without seeing Brent and Faith and the rest of her friends.

"It sounds perfect," she said.

"Give Faith a kiss for us," Reece added. "We'll see you in the morning. I'll probably have to buy this one a few more beers if she's gonna believe that I can lead as good as you can," he added, hooking his thumb toward Jenna.

Brent chuckled. "Whatever works, man."

"Too many more beers, and you'll be carrying me onto the dance floor," Jenna said, in words that proved to be unfortunately prophetic.

She'd planned ahead for dancing, so she was wearing cowboy boots instead of heels, but even so, she wobbled a little on the way to Blue, Reece's truck. Not that he ever called it that—he swore it was silly to name a car—but Jenna and Blue had an understanding.

"You okay to drive?" she asked as she climbed in.

The corner of his mouth twitched. "I'll manage," he said, and she remembered that he was tonight's designated driver and hadn't touched a drop. That was okay. She'd drunk enough for the both of them.

She'd thought that she'd sober up a bit on the drive, but there was no traffic, and it was only a few miles from Sixth Street to the well-known dance hall on South Lamar. She leaned her head against the window and watched the scenery go by. The new construction downtown. The river glowing in the moonlight. The food trucks and small boutiques that had popped up south of the river.

The cool window on her forehead revived her some-what, but she was still buzzed—and a little nauseous—when they arrived. By the time they'd pushed through the crowd and found Amanda and her guy-of-the-week, Jenna all but pounced on the basket of French fries that sat in the center of the table.

"Help yourself," Amanda said between bouts of laughter.

"She's a little lit," Reece said.

"Ya think?"

Jenna scowled at them both. "I'm Jenna," she said,

introducing herself to the dark-haired guy with the chiseled jaw who sat beside her friend.

"Easton," he said, in an accent she couldn't place, but that she thought might be from the Northeast. "Great to meet you. Sorry it's right before you're leaving."

"My big send off," she said.

Lawyer, Amanda mouthed, when Easton turned to shake hands with Reece. She waggled her eyes, and Jenna was still laughing when the men turned back.

"Something funny?" Reece asked.

"Nope," Jenna said, sharing a quick grin with Amanda before grabbing Reece's hand. "Let's dance."

"Whatever the lady wants," Reece said, then nodded at Easton. "You two coming?"

"I grew up in Connecticut, and even with four years of undergrad and three years of law school in Austin, I still can't manage the two-step."

"We won't hold that against you," Amanda said. "Come on. I can lead."

Easton went without further protest, which scored him bonus points as far as Jenna was concerned. Maybe Amanda had found a good one.

As for her and Reece, any lingering disappointment that Brent couldn't be there faded within seconds of hitting the dance floor. Technically, Jenna supposed that Brent was the better dancer of the two. But in Reece's arms it didn't matter, because despite her tendency to trip over her own feet, she felt on fire, suddenly certain that she couldn't miss a step even if she tried.

Somehow, they fit, and with his hand firmly at her back, they moved in a silent, perfect rhythm that had her heart beating and her body thrumming. From exertion, of course—what else could it be?—but even so, when they'd finally exhausted themselves and stopped for a drink, she stepped away quickly, a little unnerved by how much she didn't want to break contact.

The first beer barely quenched her thirst, and over the next hour, she drank another—possibly two—then sat and watched the room spin while Easton went off to find food, and Reece invited Amanda out onto the floor.

Jenna watched them, her jaw aching until she realized she was clenching her teeth and forced herself to relax.

What the hell was wrong with her? Amanda loved to dance, and Easton didn't know the steps. Of course she wanted to dance with Reece.

"How long have you two been going out?" Easton asked, returning to the table with a fresh basket of fries and a plate of chicken fried steak.

"What? Oh, no. We're just friend. Best friends."

"Really? I just assumed—"

"Friends," she said firmly, pulling her hand back instead of grabbing some fries. Suddenly, her stomach felt a little too jumpy for food. Instead, she snatched up the whiskey from one of the four Two-Steps—beer with a whiskey chaser—that Easton had ordered after the last round of beer. She slammed back the whiskey, ignoring the beer. She didn't need the extra dose of alcohol—Lord knew she was buzzed enough already. But she wanted it. Wanted to be numb. Anesthetized. Wanted to not feel whatever she was feeling. The sweet prickle of sensation when Reece touched her. The tight curl of jealousy when he held Amanda.

It had to be melancholy. A departure-induced yearning that had infiltrated her consciousness. Because even though she was excited about her job, she also didn't want to leave. Or, more accurately, she didn't want to leave Reece.

She sat bolt upright as the impact of the errant thought hit her. Reece?

No, no, no. Reece *and* Brent. She voiced the words clearly in her head, because right then, correcting her unspoken mistake was the most important thing in the world. Reece. And. Brent.

That's what she'd meant, of course. Her thoughts were all muddled. She just didn't want to leave her friends and go off alone to the big city. But at the same time, she did. The job was a dream, and it's not like she'd stay away forever.

Would she?

She frowned, her eyes on Reece as she considered. She'd always thought that she'd get experience elsewhere, then come back to Austin. But why? She wanted to plan large-scale events, and didn't that mean that Los Angeles was her target market?

Maybe, she thought, as Reece dipped Amanda. But maybe there were reasons to come back, too.

Mentally, she groaned. Her thoughts were going in circles. So much so that she didn't even notice when Easton cut in, pulling Amanda into his arms. Moments later, Reece was beside Jenna, tugging her to her feet.

"You're fading, kid. I should get you home."

The band finished the song, and Reece raised his hand to call Amanda and Easton over to say goodbye. But then the music started up again, probably from the jukebox. Not the fast rhythm of a Texas two-step, but the easy melody of a slow dance. "Wait," she said, squeezing his hand and urging him onto the floor. "I love this song."

"You need—"

But she didn't let him finish. She pressed against him, her arms going around his neck, her cheek tucked in against his shoulder. With a sigh, she breathed in the scent of him, all musk and male and beer.

"Jenna—" He cut himself off, his voice tight, as if her name were ice and about to crack.

"Mmm?" She snuggled closer, a warm glow filling her, and after a moment, his arms tightened around her, pulling her closer until she could feel every inch of his tight, hard muscles as they swayed in time with the strains of George Strait's *The Chair*. And for one moment—one blissful, wonderful, amazing moment—the entire world seemed perfect.

Then he shifted and reality crashed around her again. "Jenna." He seemed to be choking on her name. She looked up, confused, and saw a mixture of determination and fluster in the lines of his face. The song wasn't quite over, but he pushed her away. "We need to get you home."

"No, I—"

"Have a huge day tomorrow and need sleep." He hooked a finger under her chin, and she saw steely deter-mination etched on his face. "You're wasted, kiddo."

"I am." The words felt like they were oozing out of her. "But it's okay." She smiled up at him. "You're here to take care of me."

His throat moved as he swallowed. "Hell yeah, I am. Come on," he added, leading her off the dance floor. "You need sleep and aspirin and water. You don't want to drive all the way to Van Horn tomorrow with the monster of all hangovers."

"It may be too late for that," she said, as the room did a very unpleasant tilting thing. "I think I'm going to be sick."

"Bathroom," he said, and started leading her there. She grabbed his arm, struggling to stay upright, because the floor had started rolling now. Her stomach, however, had settled.

"Actually, I want to go home," she said, because the

idea of kneeling on the floor in a public bathroom and puking up her guts sounded miserable. "I think it'll pass."

"You're sure?" He peered at her, and she felt a bit like a ticking bomb. "You're not going to barf in the truck, are you?"

"Soil Blue? Never."

A hint of a grin touched his lips, and he nodded. They found Amanda and Easton to say goodbye, though the parting wasn't much more than a gray blur to Jenna. And once she was settled in the truck, she closed her eyes and let the rhythm of the road lull her into a semi-sleep state, where memories of slow-dancing with Reece mixed with fantasies of soft kisses and gentle caresses.

She moaned and squirmed, some part of her mind knowing that those kinds of thoughts would only lead to trouble, and another part of her mind thinking that she didn't care. That this electric sizzle now burning through her was worth it, and that she'd never felt safer than she did right now, with his arms tight around her and his breath soft against her face, and—

Right now?

Her eyes flew open, and she realized she was no longer in the truck. Instead, she was cradled in his arms as he climbed the stairs to her second-floor apartment in Austin's Tarrytown neighborhood. She squirmed, trying to get free, because as it was, she liked the feel of his arms more than she wanted to. "I can walk," she protested. "I'm fine."

"Sure you are," he said. "I'm just trying to get in a full workout today."

She made a face, squirmed some more, and gave up. They'd reached her door anyway, and he shifted his grip, then punched in the unlock code. A moment later, she was on her couch.

And a moment after that, she was bolting for the bathroom.

She didn't make it. Her stomach revolted, she fell to her knees, and because she was trying not to mess up her carpet, she ended up vomiting all over her shirt and jeans.

"Oh, baby, it's okay." Like magic, Reece was beside her, wrapping one of her oversized towels around her to keep the mess at bay, and then leading her into the bathroom. Where, of course, her stomach decided to have another go. This time, at least, she managed to hug the toilet, and Reece even held her hair out of the way.

When it passed, she drooped to the floor and rested her face on the cold hard tile, then sighed with pleasure.

"Oh, no, sweetheart." His gentle voice roused her, and she peeled open her eyes to find him unbuttoning the slate gray shirt he was wearing.

"What are you—"

"Needs to be laundered," he said, tossing it aside, and pulling off the damp T-shirt underneath, too.

Her chest tightened, and a powerful wave of longing crashed over her. It didn't make sense. She'd seen him without his shirt dozens of times. Hundreds, maybe. And the sight of his bare chest had never left her fluttery. Those tight muscles; that vibrant ink. Never before had she longed to stroke his warm skin. To feel his heartbeat under her fingertips.

But she wanted to now, dammit.

She closed her eyes, her stomach roiling. "Oh, God. Sorry. I'm so, so sorry."

"Hey, no worries," he said, thankfully misunderstanding. "But we need to get you cleaned up. Come on."

But *coming on* wasn't something her body wanted to do. Or her head, for that matter. All she wanted was to stay on the floor and clutch the ground until it stopped spinning.

She tried to tell him that, but apparently she'd forgotten how to speak. And when she tried to open her eyes, it turns out she'd forgotten how to do that, too.

Her mind knew what was going on—knew that he'd started the shower, knew that he was undressing her—but she was utterly incapable of commenting on that interesting fact.

And time seemed to be jumping around, too, no longer obeying basic rules of physics, because then she was standing, and water was sluicing over her bare skin, and Reece's arm was around her, his skin hot against hers as he used his other hand to gently rinse her off. A wild tremor ran through her, her body betraying her as she craved a more intimate touch. His fingertip stroking her breast, then following the droplets of water down lower and lower until this entire surreal night exploded into pleasure in his arms.

It would be so easy. All she had to do was conjure the words. Tell him. *Beg him.*

No. Oh, God, what was she thinking?

Thinking? What was she *feeling*? This was Reece. This was innocent.

This was her body talking when her mind knew better, all because she'd drunk too damn much.

Her mind flipped again, and he was drying her off and helping her into her favorite fuzzy robe. Then she was in bed, curled up next to him, still cocooned in the robe.

"I've got you," he murmured. "Just try to sleep."

She answered, her voice muddy. Thanking him. Telling him she loved him. That she'd miss him. That she was so sorry she'd ruined their last night out.

But he just brushed her cheek and told her to hush. She didn't. Instead, she looked up at him, her mouth pulling into a smile. "I like it," she said, reaching out to rub her palm over his newly shaved head. His skin felt cool and smooth. "It suits you."

"You think?"

She pushed herself up onto her knees, feeling a little wobbly, then bent and kissed his head. "For luck, okay?" She pulled back, looking earnestly into his eyes. For a second, she thought she saw a burning ember, but then the moment passed, and she felt the heavy weight of disappointment fill her.

"You need to sleep," he said firmly, as she sagged back against the pillows, her body surrendering to exhaustion. Then he pulled her blanket up and stroked her hair, and the touch soothed her even as it sent shivers coursing down her spine.

Sleep was drawing her under, pulling her down into the dark. But she didn't want to go. She wanted more. Him. His body hard and heavy above her. His mouth tasting every inch of her.

She wanted the fantasy turned to reality.

But she couldn't have it, and so she kept her mouth shut and her eyes closed tight and surrendered to the lure of sleep, afraid that if she looked at him, he'd see her desire.

Then everything would change, and she'd lose her friend forever.

And that was something that she'd never, ever let happen.

Chapter Five

JENNA WOKE in a tangle of sweaty sheets and lingering dreams so wicked she feared she might set the bed on fire. She blinked, trying to remember the details, knowing only that her mind had been filled with Reece, and telling herself that she was allowed only a few more minutes to savor the heat before she locked the dreams away in the vault and never, ever spoke of them.

A quick rap on the bedroom door made her squeal, and she sat up, pulling her hand out of her panties as she did and biting her lower lip with mortification.

And with frustration, too. She *really* wished she could remember some specifics.

"Jenna?" Brent's voice filtered through the door. "You up?"

"Yeah," she called. "Well, I am now."

"Sorry. But it's time to rise and shine. Breakfast with Reece, remember?"

She groaned.

"You okay?"

"I'm fine," she called, climbing out of bed and putting

on the bathrobe he'd set out for her. She padded across the room and opened the door, revealing a sweat-slicked Brent, shirtless and fresh from his morning run. "I feel like I've only slept for an hour," she continued. "Oh, wait. I pretty much *have* only slept for an hour."

"A few minutes more than that," he said wryly.

"One or two, maybe." She looked him up and down. "You look far too awake."

"Curse of the job," he said. "Well, the job plus parenthood."

"Which means that this morning you've already taken Faith to school, gotten in a run, and answered at least a half dozen emails. I feel like a slug."

"You don't look like one." He nodded toward the attached bathroom. "Go ahead and take a shower. You'll feel better."

She eyed him. "Don't you want to get cleaned up and dressed before Reece gets here?"

"We've got time. I'll grab my clothes and go shower and shave in Faith's bathroom."

"You're shaving your beard?" She hoped not. It wasn't heavy, and she liked the way it defined his jaw.

"No, just cleaning it up. Part shave, part trimming."

"Good. But I can shower in there if you'd rather. I peeked in last night, and Faith's bathroom has a serious pink theme going."

"I'm man enough to handle it," he teased. "Besides, I'm guessing all your makeup is already laid out in there." He nodded toward the master bathroom.

She shrugged, sheepish. "We have *so* known each other too long."

His grin flickered. "I'll take Faith's bathroom. Go on and take your shower."

"Fine." She headed toward the bathroom, then paused

and turned back. "But shave in here, okay? I don't think any little girl wants to see daddy whiskers in her girlie pink bathroom."

"Fair enough," he said, then grabbed some jeans and a T-shirt out of his dresser and headed into the hall.

She was showered and back in the robe when he returned and knocked on the bathroom door, now wearing jeans and no shirt, presumably so he could shave without worrying about his clothes.

"All yours," she said, grabbing her hairbrush and heading into the bedroom to rummage in her suitcase. The clock said eight forty-five. Reece was coming at nine, and she had a job interview at eleven. She'd packed a dress for today, but in her discombobulated state last night, she hadn't hung it up. Now, of course, it was a wrinkled mess, and she didn't have time to iron, have breakfast with the guys, and get across town to the interview on time.

Frowning, she laid the dress out on the bed as she eyed the bathroom, thinking that she'd turn the shower on full blast and steam the wrinkles away as soon as Brent was out of there. In the meantime, maybe a little coffee would dissolve the rest of the cobwebs in her head.

With a quick tug on the sash to tighten her robe, she moved into the hallway that led to the kitchen. As she passed the living room, the front door opened, and Reece walked in, calling out, "Hey, I'm here," and then stopping short when his gaze landed on her.

Jenna froze, last night's fantasies and dreams rushing back to her—along with the awkward realization that she was naked under her robe. A completely uninteresting fact five minutes ago, now it seemed like the most important thing in the world.

"Hi," she said, her hand rising to hold the neck of the

robe together. "So, um, hey." God, she sounded like an idiot. "Aren't you early?"

"A little. That a problem?" He took a step toward her, his brows knit and his mouth a thin line. He looked confused, and why wouldn't he be? When had any of the three of them ever cared if the others were early?

"Duh. No. It was just an observation. Um, I was just about to put on some coffee. Want some?" Her smile felt wobbly, and she hurried into the kitchen, wishing that she could pull the fantasies out of her head, crumple them up, and throw them away. Barring that, she wished that she could at least act normal.

He followed her into the kitchen, then leaned against the pantry door, still looking wary. She opened the cupboard then said a silent thank you that Brent didn't have any beans ground. It gave her an excuse to fill the grinder, turn the gizmo on, and *think*.

When she released the button and the racket stopped, she turned back to Reece just in time to see his eyes go wide. He was looking down the hallway at something outside her line of sight, and she stepped around the counter so she could see what had caught his eye.

The *what* was Brent, coming toward them as he pulled a T-shirt over his head, a dab of shaving cream still on his face. "About your dress on the bed," he was saying. "Do you want me to hang it up for you?" His head emerged, and he looked at Reece with surprise. "Oh, hey. I didn't know you were here alread—"

But that was all he said. Because the next second, Reece's fist flew out and landed—*pow!*—on Brent's jaw.

Chapter Six

REECE PULLED HIS ARM BACK, appalled by what he'd just done—and at the same time, certain he'd do it again in a heartbeat.

"Reece!" Jenna's scream cut through the rage and jealousy and betrayal that clung to him like mist. He turned to see her staring him down, Brent's robe tight around her body. She was probably naked underneath, and the image of Brent's hands on her filled his mind. Brent stroking her, taking advantage.

Taking what was his.

No. Reece clenched his fist again, this time as much in defense against his own thoughts as against the fury that still bubbled inside him.

"Christ, man." Brent rubbed his jaw, manipulating it from side to side like he was checking for broken bones. "What the hell was that for?"

"We're supposed to be watching out for her, not fucking her."

"Have you lost your mind? We haven't—"

"Watching out for me?" Jenna's voice rose with indignation. "Who elected you to the posse?" She stepped in front of him, her back to Brent. "Because in case you missed the memo, I can sleep with whoever I want to."

Bile rose in Reece's throat. *He'd been right. Oh, holy fuck, he'd been right.*

"And what the hell do you think you're doing coming in here like a warden and throwing punches?" She took another step and got right in his face, so close he could count her freckles, dark against her pale, angry skin. He was struck by an overwhelming urge to taste each one. Either that or grab her by the arms and shake her.

Or maybe he should gather her up, kiss her hard, and show her once and for all whose bed she belonged in, because, goddammit, if he'd known that Brent would—

"And how is who I sleep with any of your business?" Jenna continued, interrupting the barrage of thoughts that burst through his mind like machine gun fire. "Did I say anything about Megan? Or about the dozens of women before her?"

She had, actually. He distinctly remembered her standing in much the same posture and telling him time and again that he needed to get his shit together, because the way he was going, he'd have dated every woman in Travis County. Of course, she'd been wearing jeans that day. Not a bathrobe.

He drew in a breath and tried to keep his temper in check. "This isn't about—"

"This isn't about anything," Brent interrupted, using the same voice that Reece had heard him use with Faith when she was being particularly cranky. "Jenna slept in my bed, I slept on the couch, and I'm guessing nobody's sleeping with you lately. Because you, my friend, are wound too tight."

"What the hell, Reece?" Jenna snapped. "Do you

honestly think I'd sleep with Brent? And right down the hall from his daughter?"

"You told me you were staying with Amanda."

She rolled her eyes, then turned and started walking toward the kitchen. "Oh, right." She paused in the doorway and looked back over her shoulder at him. "And since I'm not allowed to change my plans without sending you a text message asking permission, I'm in trouble now."

"Dammit, Jenna—"

She whirled on him. "Don't 'dammit, Jenna,' me. Unless I'm camped out on your couch, it's none of your business where I sleep. But for your information, the Franklins are having their floors redone, so Amanda's got her parents in her house. And I wasn't keen on sleeping on the sofa while Mr. Franklin hangs out in the living room at five in the morning watching the news."

"Children," Brent said, "if we could just—"

"Oh, no," Jenna said, cutting Brent off. Apparently, she was still on a very Jenna-like roll. She turned her attention back to Reece. "You seriously thought we'd slept together? You guys are my best friends. You know that. Hell, you're my family, and you know that, too. Besides, I don't think about him that way," she continued, her voice tight and sharp. "But even if I did, do you think I'd risk that? Risk losing the only family I have besides my mom? Damn you, Reece Walker. You're a goddamn idiot."

She was right, of course. He didn't believe it, but damned if an insane rush of jealousy hadn't completely swept him away in a tidal wave of primal, raw emotion.

He couldn't remember a time he'd lost his shit like that, and all he could do now was shake his head, apologize, and hope there wasn't a big neon sign flashing over his head advertising exactly why he'd gotten so bent out of shape in the first place.

"I'm an ass, okay? That's the bottom line, and the sooner we all accept the truth, the happier we'll all be."

"An ass," she repeated, leaning casually against the doorframe. "Care to elucidate?"

"I think he's summed it up nicely," Brent said. Jenna turned to him, her arms crossed and her mouth a thin line of disapproval. She stared him down. One second, then another—and then all three of them burst into laughter.

"Oh, shit," Jenna said. "I mean, seriously, Reece. What the fuck?"

"Sorry. I know." He ran his palm over his head, wishing the contact could help him come up with something even remotely plausible. "It's this bullshit with Tyree. I didn't sleep for thinking about it, and then I walked in and—well, straw, meet camel."

Her mouth twisted with exasperation as she pushed away from the wall. "Idiot," she muttered, then hip-butted him as she moved past him into the kitchen. She paused long enough to point to Brent. "You, go finish getting dressed. And to answer your question, yes, you can hang up my dress. In the bathroom, with the shower on hot. I need to steam out some wrinkles. And as for you..."

She turned her attention to Reece. "Make some coffee, would you? I'll start bacon, and Brent can do the eggs when he gets back."

Reece did as she said, and when the coffee was brewing, he hoisted himself up on the counter and watched as she poked at the frying bacon with the tongs. Her back was to him, and he could just make out the curves of her ass against the thick material of the robe. He wanted to slide off the cabinet, go to her, and cup her ass in his hands as he bent to kiss her neck. She probably tasted like bacon. Either way, he could damn sure eat her up.

And no way could that ever happen, for all the reasons she'd stated.

As if he'd spoken aloud, she looked over her shoulder, her brows rising in question. "Yeah?"

"Just watching you cook and thinking."

"Oh? About what?" She turned back to the sizzling pan, moving the meat around, as he hopped down and came up behind her.

What was he thinking? The truth was something he couldn't tell her, especially after her announcement that she considered him only family, and didn't think of him *that* way at all.

The truth was that he was thinking about her. About the feel of her skin that night. And he was trying to remember the exact pinkish-brown of her exposed areola when he'd undressed her. And he was probably heading straight for hell because those thoughts spun into a sweet fantasy about sliding his hand between her thighs to cup her smooth, shaved pussy. Not to mention the X-rated movie playing in his mind about what would have happened had he not simply cleaned her up that night, but if he'd laid her naked on the bed then tasted every warm, delicious inch of her.

But those weren't best friend thoughts, and so as he moved behind her now in Brent's kitchen, he said none of it. Instead, he told her he was thinking about bacon.

"Bacon?" She didn't sound convinced, but he didn't have the strength to argue, not when he was right behind her, the scent of her shampoo intoxicating him. Brent's shampoo, actually, but it smelled one hell of a lot better on Jenna.

"I'm ravenous." He leaned to one side, his hand resting on the stainless steel edge of the stove as he reached around her with his other hand to snag a piece of bacon off the paper-towel covered plate onto which she was piling the cooked pieces. He paused in the motion, realizing that she was effectively caged in his arms, and it would be so ridiculously easy to brush her hair with his lips, or even spin her around and capture her mouth before she could protest.

"Reece." Her back was still to him, so he couldn't see her face, but he heard an unfamiliar tightness in her voice. An awareness. A heat. And he felt a corresponding tension in his balls.

"What?" He stepped closer under the guise of getting another slice of bacon, and in the process his chest brushed her back. For just an instant, time froze. And in that infinite moment, he felt the fire of a future he craved —and remembered one simple, wonderful, confusing point: she'd said she didn't think of *him* that way. Not *them* —not Brent *and* Reece—just *him*.

And in the context of that particular conversation, the "him" in question had been Brent.

Did that mean she thought about Reece that way? As more than a friend, and definitely not family?

And even if she did, so what? She was right, after all. How could either of them risk their friendship for something that might be fun, but wouldn't last? Because he knew better than to believe relationships last. He was walking, talking proof that they didn't.

"Reece?"

"Hmm?"

"Can you move?" she asked, breaking the spell. "You're blocking me, and I'm desperate for a cup of coffee."

"What? Oh, yeah." He stepped aside, then watched as she poured a cup for herself, then passed one to him. "I really am sorry."

She took a sip, then lifted a shoulder. The robe swallowed her, and with her long hair parted in the middle, no makeup, and bare feet, she reminded him of a little girl at Christmas sipping cocoa. That illusion, however, faded when those eyes flashed green fire in his direction.

"There are a lot of jerks out there you could have saved me from over the years. But you should know that Brent isn't one of them. I mean, what were you thinking?"

"I'm pretty sure we've already established that I wasn't. Thinking, I mean." He pointed at the stove. "Go. Cook."

"Set the table," she ordered as Brent arrived and went to work on the eggs. It was a routine they'd been through at least a hundred times. And when they each had a plate and were settled at the table, Jenna nodded at Brent. "So what are we going to do about Tyree. And, yeah, I mean *we*. I know I've been gone for ages and don't work there anymore, but I love him, too. So?" she demanded, looking at them both in turn. "What's the plan?"

"We need to know the problem before the plan," Reece said. "And I mean the details of the problem. More than just the fact that he owes money."

"Must be a shit ton of money," Brent said. "Austin commercial real estate isn't cheap, and it wasn't when Tyree bought the place, either. I don't know what he paid for The Fix, but I do know the down-payment wasn't huge."

"So you're saying it's a done deal?" Jenna pressed. She reached for the salt, the sleeve of her robe brushing Reece's arm.

"I'm saying that unless Tyree's been burying gold in his backyard, he's going to need a creative solution."

"We," she corrected, looking at Reece. "Right?"

"Hell, yes," he said. No way in hell was he letting Tyree lose The Fix. Not if there was anything he could do about

it. Seeing Jenna's pleased smile at his quick reply was just a
bonus. "This is Tyree, after all."

"I know," Brent said, his expression sober. He let out a
frustrated sigh and sat back in his chair, his eyes on Reece.
"He's like us. He's practically family."

Reece swallowed, his throat thick as it always was when
he thought of his Uncle Vincent, a solider who'd died in
Afghanistan at thirty-one, leaving three-year-old Mike and
a young wife behind. Vincent Walker was Reece's father's
only brother, a surprise who'd been born when Reece's
dad, Charlie Walker, was fifteen. Also a serviceman,
Charlie had served in Desert Storm, where one of the men
in his command had been a green eighteen-year-old
named Tyree. Years later, Tyree took Vincent under his
wing and stayed with the mortally wounded younger man
in the field despite the danger to himself from continuing
enemy fire.

Reece had grown up knowing Tyree and thinking of
him as family, which meant that he was family to Brent
and Jenna, too. The three had urged him to take the
plunge when he bought The Fix, and Reece and Jenna had
been two of his first employees, with Jenna waiting tables
and Reece tending bar before he worked his way up to
manager.

Brent was still a cop back then, but he worked security
during his off-hours, ultimately quitting the force to work
at The Fix full time.

So, yeah. The Fix was home, and Tyree was family.

Helping him was a no-brainer. The question was how.

"Hard to say until we know exactly how much he
owes," Brent said when Jenna voiced that very question.
"But lending him the money seems like a good idea."

"Which he wouldn't take," Reece said. "The man's got
pride. And unless you have some gold in *your* backyard, I

don't know where we'd find the money to make it happen anyway."

"We could talk to Easton," Jenna said, referring to Amanda's former boyfriend who'd become a regular at the bar.

"If he's got too much pride to borrow from one of us, he's not going to borrow from one of the regulars," Brent said.

"Too bad," Reece said. "Some of our regulars have enough money they could just write a check. Hell, Cameron's sister won a Grammy, and she loves the place."

"Tyree would never forgive us if we started asking the customers. Same goes for one of those online crowd-funding deals. Not his style, and you know it."

"Yeah, I do," Reece admitted.

"That's not what I meant, anyway," Jenna said. "It's just that Easton's a lawyer, so he'd know how to renegotiate the loan or get an extension or forgiveness, or whatever you call it. And he knows everyone, too. Maybe whatever bank holds the note is already a client."

"Well, it's not going to do us any good to sit around making suggestions," Reece said. "We need to go talk to the man."

"Be persuasive. You have to convince him to let you help." They rose, and Jenna took all their plates and carried them to the counter, then came back. "You guys will figure something out."

She leaned in and kissed Brent's cheek, then turned to Reece. She hesitated for just a second, the pause so brief he barely noticed. Probably wouldn't have, except that he was hyperaware of her. And so he noticed the hint of a blush on her cheeks, too, when she brushed a feather-soft kiss across his cheek.

"So," she said, then cleared her throat. "Right, well, I

need to go get dressed. I've got that job interview. Wish me luck?"

"Always," Reece said.

"You don't need luck," Brent said. "You've got talent." He turned to Reece. "Ready?"

"What? Ready to tell a man I've respected my whole life, who has more pride in his little finger than you and me put together, that I know he's hurting for money just a few years before his only son's about to go off to college? Why the hell would you think I'm not ready?"

Brent met Jenna's eyes. "We'll be leaving now."

"We'll call you later to see how your interview went," Reece said.

She waved the words away. "Oh, please. Don't worry about me today. I'm just looking for a job. You guys are trying to help Tyree with his life."

Chapter Seven

IT WAS a twenty-minute drive from Brent's north-central bungalow to Tyree's East Austin home in the Wilshire Wood neighborhood. But for the entire trek, neither Brent nor Reece said a word to each other. Instead, the only sound was a stream of music from KUTX, a local station owned by the University that aired an eclectic mix of music including local artists. Normally, Reece wouldn't mind—part of his job was bringing in local talent, and he'd found several bands for the club by tuning in.

This morning, however, the music-filled silence seemed heavy. And it wasn't until Brent had pulled up in front of the charming stone house and killed the engine that he turned to Reece and spoke.

"Be careful," he said, then opened the door and slipped out of the Volvo before Reece could ask what the hell he meant.

Except, of course, he didn't have to ask. Reece and Brent had been friends a long time, and he knew damn well that Brent wasn't a guy who missed much. It's one of the things that made him such a good father.

It was also damned annoying, and when Faith was a teenager, Reece was pretty sure she'd back him up on that.

"You're imagining things," he said as they walked up the sidewalk, the concrete uneven from years of tree roots pressing upward.

"Could be," Brent said easily, then rang the doorbell. "It's happened before." He stood back, leaning against the stone facade, his brown eyes fixed on Reece. "But in my imaginary world, you're not exactly Mr. Commitment. And Jenna needs a friend more than she needs another guy who disappears on her."

"You don't know what you're talking about," Reece protested, though it sounded hollow even to his own ears. "And anyway, if you think that I would *ever* hurt—"

The door flew open, cutting off his words, and Elijah Johnson stood there, tall and lanky in a suit and tie. Half-black and half-Japanese, his skin was a shade lighter than Tyree's, and he'd inherited his mother's eyes and his father's broad shoulders. In the last year, the kid had shot up, surpassing his father in height. And even though Reece had seen him only a few weeks ago, it seemed like the kid had grown another foot since then.

"Isn't it a school day?" Brent asked. "And why are you in a suit? You look snappy, by the way."

"Yeah? Is snappy professional? I need to look professional." He took a step back, then waved his hands to indicate the whole outfit as he looked between the two of them. "Would you hire me?"

"Hell, yeah," Reece said. "What am I hiring you for?"

"My boy's got an interview in about an hour over at Dell Children's Hospital." Tyree's deep voice came from the side of the house, and Reece turned to see his friend and boss come up the driveway in sweatpants and a white T-shirt that displayed bulging muscles and tattooed arms.

His dark skin glistened, and he wore fingerless leather gloves. He'd obviously been working out in the makeshift gym that took up one half of the detached two-car garage.

"An interview?" Brent said. "Let me guess. Neuro-surgeon."

Eli rolled his eyes, then stepped back, holding the door so that the two visitors could come in, followed by Tyree. "It's for a summer internship in the lab. And if I get it, then I'd work there first and second period my senior year."

Tyree practically beamed. "My boy's decided he wants to go to med school." His smooth baritone voice was usually laced with a hint of his Cajun background. Today, it was also filled with pride. "An internship like this could open some doors."

"I'm one of five candidates. There's only two slots, so we're down to the wire." The kid grimaced as he looked at Brent and Reece. "So, you think it's okay? Like, you're not just being nice? Dad says so, but he can be lame, and—"

"You'll knock it out of the park," Reece assured him.

"Thanks a lot," Tyree protested, cuffing his son's upper arm.

Eli exhaled loudly. "Okay. Right. Well, I'm going, then."

"Is this a bad time?" Brent asked Tyree. "If you need to drive him..."

"I'm walking," Eli said. "It's only a few blocks, and, you know, nerves."

"You sure?" Reece said, but no one was listening. Tyree was pulling his son into a bear hug.

"Just be yourself, my man. Your mom would be proud."

"I'll text you after," he said, then set off down the street, his headphones in and his feet moving in time with the music.

"Med school," Tyree said, shaking his head as his son disappeared. He ushered Reece and Brent in the rest of the way, then shut the door behind them. "Hard to believe. I mean, this is the same kid I was afraid was going to drop out of school or join a gang just a few years ago. And now he has his heart set on med school. Not to mention the grades to get him into a first-rate pre-med program."

"You've done a good job with him," Reece said. "Teiko would be proud." Elijah's mother had died from complications following a brutal car wreck, and the tragedy had taken a huge toll on the family. On Reece, too. Tyree and Teiko's marriage was one of the few functional marriages he'd ever witnessed, and the death of that sweet, stubborn woman had felt like a kick in the gut to Reece. He could only imagine how much pain Tyree had endured.

"It was touch and go there for a while," Tyree said as they settled at the table, just like they always did to shoot the shit, play cards, or talk about work. "But I think the kid's turning out okay."

"Hell, yeah, he is," Brent added.

"But med school." Tyree whistled, then leaned back, his fingers interlaced behind his head. "That boy better hope he gets a scholarship."

Brent shot Reece a meaningful glance, which Tyree must have noticed because he sat up straighter. "All right," he said. "This obviously isn't a social call. What's this about?" The casual tone was gone, replaced by the no-nonsense voice of a business owner talking to his employees.

"You tell us," Brent said.

"Like that, is it?" He stood up, then crossed to the fridge and pulled out a protein shake. Tyree was a big man, all muscle, and he'd spent the better part of his life in the military. And a good portion of those years in command of other men. He could be damned intimidating when it suited him. Apparently, it suited him now, because Reece was beginning to feel like he was one of Tyree's troops getting dressed down for breaking formation.

"The way I see it, you either came to talk about something personal or about work. If it's personal, then you're going to have to tell me what's on your mind, because I don't have a clue. And if you came to talk about work—well, if that's the case, I might have some idea why you came. But I also know it's none of your damn business."

"Ty—"

The older man pointed a finger at Reece. "None of your damn business," he repeated. "Now I think you boys should go. I've got some things to do before opening The Fix at two."

Reece shot a look at Brent, who lifted a shoulder in a *the hell with that* kind of way.

"That might be true," Reece began, leaning back in his chair and stretching out his long legs, "if we were just your employees. But seems to me we're more like family. Or are you going to tell me I'm wrong?"

"What I should tell you is that your daddy raised you better than to stick your nose in where it's not welcome. This is my problem, not yours."

"It's our problem if The Fix goes out of business," Reece said.

"And it's our problem if a friend's in trouble," Brent added.

"Dammit, Ty, forget your pride. You don't have to handle every crisis on your own. Tell us what's going on and give us the chance to help you."

"Anyone ever tell you that you're an insolent son-of-a-bitch?"

"All the time." Reece punctuated his grin with a quick lift of his brows. "So?"

"Ah, hell." Tyree put the shake back in the fridge, then pulled out three beers. He glanced at the clock—just creeping up on eleven—and shrugged. "If we're going to do this, we're going to do it right."

He reached for the can opener he kept in a construction-paper and glitter-decorated coffee can that had a place of prominence in the middle of the table. The paper was pink, and the glitter was glued on in some approximation of bunny shapes. Possibly horses. But since Reece knew the artist personally and had a similar piece of artwork on his kitchen counter, his money was on bunnies. Last Christmas, Faith had been all about the bunnies.

"What do you think you know?" Tyree demanded, opening the three beers in turn.

"That you're staring down a barrel. The balance of a mortgage due at the end of the year. What I don't know is how much that loan is. But you've been acting off the last couple of days, so I'm thinking it's more than you've got tucked away in the cookie jar."

"You're thinking along the right lines," Tyree said, his voice gruff.

"How much?" Brent demanded boldly.

Tyree exhaled, then scrubbed his palms over his face. "Too fucking much," he said, and when he told them the actual number, Reece had to agree. From the way Brent sat up, his posture turning just a little too stiff, it looked like Brent thought so, too.

"Downtown Austin real estate ain't cheap," Tyree said, "and there was no way I wasn't going to get my place. You boys already know this, but that was always my dream. A bar. Maybe a food truck—you know me and my kitchen. But I wanted it to be more about the eats, even more about the drink. I wanted it to be a destination. I wanted a place that folks thought of almost like a home. Not like they were visiting, but like it was theirs, you know?"

"You know we do. And we've got some damn loyal customers who think just that way. They'd help you out, Ty." Brent tapped a knuckle on the tabletop. "You know they would."

Ty didn't even miss a beat, just kept on with the story. "Teiko's dying wish was for me to open my place. One that hit all my high points. A place that had at-mos-phere," he said, emphasizing each syllable just the way Teiko used to do when she wanted to make a point. Then he flashed a watery smile. "Took me a while to find the place but I think she'd approve."

"I told you back then she would," Reece said softly. "Go on. You borrowed money to buy it, obviously."

Tyree sighed. "This house is paid off, and no way was I going to mortgage it. Couldn't even if I wanted to. Eli's granddaddy left it to him. A couple of years and he can kick his old man out if he wants to, once he's eighteen and it comes out of trust. We emptied our savings and got incurred a shit-ton of debt for Teiko's medical bills, but after she passed—"

His voice hitched, and he took a long swallow of beer. "Well, after she passed there was the life insurance, and I paid off the debt and put the rest in the bank. My credit was still screwed, though. Medical bills can do you in. Then when I found the property, I used the left-over life insurance for a down payment on The Fix. Seven-year term, amortized over thirty, with a huge fucking balloon at the end. With my credit in such bad shape, that was the best deal I could get, and it wasn't even with a bank. Now I'm thinking I should have just kept on walking."

"Not with a bank?"

"Buddy of mine knows a guy who put me in touch with a private lender. Venture capitalist type. All on the up-and-up, but just because he's one guy doesn't mean he won't foreclose."

"You've asked."

"I practically begged. No dice. I pay off the loan by the end of the year, or I lose the property." He shook his head, then took another swallow, finishing off the beer. "It all seemed like a long way off when I signed the papers, but in the last four years, Austin's changed. Competition's fierce. Places like Bodacious move in, and they're all tits and ass and dollar drinks. That's hard shit to compete with."

"You're preaching to the choir," Reece said. As the manager, he knew just how hard it was to attract new customers, especially when the college students tended toward the chain bars with the all-night happy hours. "But we have something those dollar traps like Bodacious don't —a loyal customer base."

"That only goes so far," Ty said.

"Could go further," Brent put in, obviously following Reece's train of thought. "Let us talk to a few people. It might be possible for us to pull together enough money to pay off the original loan with a new one from one of the regulars. I can think of a few who could write a check today."

Tyree shook his head. "No. Teiko knew that The Fix was my dream, and she wanted me to have my shot. But she wouldn't want me throwing good money after bad. It's either working, or it's not. I'm not chasing loans for the rest of my life. And I'm sure as hell not borrowing from someone I may not be able to pay back."

"Then we ask for donations. A little bit from a lot of people. It can add up."

"I appreciate the ideas, I do. But one of those Internet

campaigns? You two know that's not my style. My bar stays open because people come in for the drink and the music and the food or not at all. I didn't lose my business because of a hurricane or a fire—that's the kind of thing people donate for. To help someone hit by bad luck. But if The Fix goes under, it'll be because of good old-fashioned competition. And that's played inside the bar at the cash register, not on the Internet."

Reece met Brent's eyes. Truth was, he didn't disagree.

Slowly, Brent nodded. "Fair enough. Then we'll just have to kick it into high gear. Up the cover charge, maybe sneak up a few drink prices, but bring them in with dollar beers. And book a few A-listers. Kiki'd come play at the Fix, I'm sure," he added, referring to Cameron's sister. "We'll make it happen."

"It's a good pitch, but it's all talk," Tyree said. "You boys are just now diving into this mess. I've been living it for months. And trust me, I've done the math. To earn the money I need I'll have to charge prices that would drive away the customers. And then I can't earn the money."

"You're talking like it's over," Reece said.

"That's because it is," Ty said. "You know I'm right. I've got some feelers out for a buyer. With any luck, I'll be able to pay off the note and end up with a little cash in my pocket, too. More luck, and I'll find a buyer before the year's out who wants to keep The Fix as is. Hate to think I brought her to life, only to have her turned into the downtown Austin location of some restaurant conglomerate."

"Surely not," Brent said.

"Already got nibbles on that front. You heard of Booty Call?"

"Ah, hell no." Reece pinched the bridge of his nose.

"Same company that owns Bodacious," Tyree said,

stating a truth that Reece already knew. "Figure they're trying to lock up the block."

Brent met his eyes. "Over my dead body."

"A little extreme, but I agree with the sentiment."

"Why a buyer?" Reece asked. "Why not look for a partner? Someone with the cash to pay off the loan and take some of the burden off you. In return, they get a piece of the business."

Tyree cocked his head, then shook it slowly. "I don't know about that."

"Are you telling me you'd rather go under than bring in someone else?"

"No." He stroked his chin. "It's not an entirely crazy idea. But I wouldn't be interested in a financial partner only. Someone who was just throwing money at me hoping for a payday, then showing up disappointed if they don't make a profit in the first two weeks."

"That's not what I'm saying," Reece assured him, ignoring the way Brent was looking at him, his brow furrowed.

"If I'm in with someone, I'm in," Tyree continued. "And they need to be, too. Someone working behind the bar, in the trenches. Not on some damn pedestal looking down and counting his coins. And I sure as hell don't know where to find someone like that."

"I do," Reece said. "You're looking at him." Both men stared at him, and Reece held his breath, waiting for Tyree to shoot him down.

He didn't. Instead, all he said was, "Now why the hell would you want to go and do that for?"

Reece looked across the table at a man who was part friend, part boss, but definitely part of his extended family. "Do you honestly have to ask that? Don't you think I know you'd do the same for me? For him?" he added, nodding toward Brent.

"Reece, you can't—"

"There are a lot of things I've loved and lost," Reece interrupted, his voice firm. "Uncle Vincent. My mother. Both my stepmothers." *Jenna*, he thought, though he hadn't lost her. How could he when he'd never had her? And never would.

He pushed the thought away and met Tyree's eyes. "I don't want to add The Fix to that list. I want to do this," he added. "That place is my goddamn second home, and I am not going to watch it fail. We're getting it back in the black, and if kick-starting that plan means I toss in some cash, then that's just the way it's going to be. So don't you dare disrespect me and dismiss it out of hand."

"No," Tyree said. "I wouldn't. But I'm paying you way too much if you have that kind of money sitting around just waiting—"

He cut himself off, his head tilting in thought. And Reece knew that Tyree had figured out just where Reece would get that much cash.

"Oh, fuck no. Reece, your house? You've been saving your whole adult life to build that house. I can't ask you to do that."

"You're not asking. I'm telling. And it's not a house. It's only the dream of a house." A dream he'd had for years, ever since he managed to score a piece of lakefront property in a foreclosure sale when he was a sophomore in college. Even before that, he'd wanted to build his own home. Then once he had the land, he'd started saving in earnest, and collecting notes and sketches of just how he wanted the place to turn out.

"Sometimes it's harder to lose a dream than reality," Tyree said.

"You got that right," Brent said, with a bitter twist of his lips, and Reece would have bet the entire sum in question that Brent was thinking about Olivia, Faith's very out-of-the-picture mother.

"Brent," he began, but Brent held up a hand.

"I'm in, too," Brent said.

"You don't have to do that," Reece said.

"Oh, but I think I do." He shot a thin smile toward Tyree. "I know how much our boy here's got saved for that house, and it's not enough. Close, but not enough. Fifty-fifty," he said, then held out his hand for Reece to shake.

He didn't. Not yet. "Where are you getting the money?"

"Don't ask questions if you don't want to hear the answer."

"Dammit, Brent, you've got a little girl to look out for. You can't—"

"Can't what? Can't risk it? I don't think it's too much of a risk. Or was that impassioned speech you just made bullshit?"

"You're an asshole," Reece said, but he took Brent's still outstretched hand. "But then again, you always have been."

"Neither of you are risking anything," Tyree said, and both Reece and Brent started to volley protests. "We'll do this thing, but only on my terms, you understand? And I don't want the bar to be an albatross around either of your necks."

Reece glanced at Brent to see if his friend had a clue where Tyree was going with this, but Brent only shrugged.

"So our deadline is the end of this year. New Year's Eve. I need to see a steady profit and solid projections. Not just sufficient income to pay off the loan. I need to see real potential for growth."

"And if not?" Reece asked.

"That nibble from Booty Call's more than a nibble. It's a full-blown offer that expires the end of the year. We're not in a rock-solid position, then we accept the offer, you boys get your investments back plus a percentage, and we call it a good try and move on." He looked at both of them in turn, his arms crossed over his chest as he leaned back. "Those are my terms. Take 'em or leave 'em."

"That's not a lot of time for the kind of turn-around in income we're talking about," Reece said, thinking over inventory, personnel, the menu, and the current marketing plans. "It's already mid-April."

"We need to build buzz," Brent said. "Get the word out and get more customers in. Reece is right. That's not very long in the grand scheme of things."

"That's all the time there is," Tyree said, crossing his arms over his massive chest. "Deal's on the table. Ball's in your court."

"We're in," Reece said, shooting Brent a *trust me* look. "There's just one condition."

Tyree squinted suspiciously. "What's that?"

"We need to add one more partner to the mix."

Chapter Eight

"PARTNER?" The word tasted strange on Jenna's tongue, and she glanced sideways at Amanda, as if her friend could help interpret this paradox. They'd met at The Fix for a late lunch after Jenna's interview because, as Amanda had put it, "I love my parents, but if I don't escape, I'll turn gray before I'm thirty-five."

So Jenna had served as a helpful excuse for Amanda to get away. Amanda, however, wasn't returning the helpfulness favor; she looked just as confused as Jenna.

Jenna turned her attention back to Reece and Brent, both of whom were standing behind the bar right in front of Jen and Amanda's half-eaten order of mini crab cakes. "You're saying that you want me to be a partner in The Fix? Like an owner? That's what you're saying?"

"That's what we're saying." Reece took her glass and refilled the Diet Coke. "So?"

Her eyes cut toward the back hallway, down which Tyree had just disappeared. He'd come over with the guys, greeted both women, and then told Jenna that Brent and Reece had something to tell her. Then Tyree had left, and her two best friends had shooed Eric—the first shift bartender who'd been telling Jen and Amanda about his unsuccessful hunt for a new apartment—down to the far end of the bar.

After that, the guys had relayed their morning conversation with Tyree and the plan to get the bar back on its feet.

A plan that, frankly, she thought was brilliant. For them. For her, not so much.

"In case you missed the memo, I don't have any money to invest. I don't even have enough money to buy a car. Thus the job search and this morning's interview. Which, by the way, went fabulously, thanks for asking."

Amanda whistled through her teeth, then leaned back, giving each guy the eye. "Doghouse," she said under her breath.

Brent scowled in her direction, and Jenna rolled her eyes. Brent and Amanda had gone out twice, and even though there didn't seem to be sparks, Jenna was a romantic and still held out hope. Brent needed a woman in his life, and Faith needed a mom. And since Amanda and Brent were two of her best friends...

"So you got the job?" Reece said, interrupting her matchmaking meanderings.

"What? Oh, no. Not yet anyway. But I'm sure I will. They want me on a project tonight. They called it an on-the-job interview. So it's looking good."

"Yeah? That's terrific."

"Thanks, but I don't have it yet. And it's not like they're going to advance me the big bucks. So I'm not sure how I'm supposed to be a partner."

"We want you for your mind, not your money," Brent said, and Amanda snorted.

"Men *never* say that," Amanda muttered, then shoved another crab cake into her mouth.

Jenna swallowed a laugh. "All right. I'm listening."

"We need your marketing expertise," Brent explained. "Your ideas and your time. Not your money."

"Oh." She looked between the guys. "Really?"

"We told you our deal with Tyree. We're looking at a big project on a short fuse. We need someone who can help us get the word out. Who can increase the customer base and, well, do whatever it is you do to drum up business."

"Oh," she said again. "I can do that. But if I get this job..."

"We'll take whatever time you can give us," Brent added, leaning forward, but his urging was unnecessary. Of course she was in. This was for Tyree. And now that the guys had invested, it was for them, too. No way would she let them down. No way did she want to.

She leaned back, thinking. "My friend Maia works in marketing. An Austin friend, not LA. I'll do some brainstorming with her. And we need to see about doing a little work on the stage if we're going to bring in more acts. If we shift the angle, we can increase the size of the stage and the floor space for dancing. Double-win."

Reece flashed a wide grin—the kind that went straight to her gut and made her look away quickly. "So you're in?"

"You know I am," she said, meeting Brent's fist-bump as Reece waved to an incoming customer, then slid down the bar to take an order.

"We knew you'd come through," Brent said. "Tell Reece I'll talk to him later. I've got to go run a systems check on the security cams. Congrats again," he said. "And good luck tonight."

"Thanks," she said, reaching up to accept his hug. Then she watched as he headed to the back of the bar.

Once he'd disappeared into the hall, she turned her attention to Amanda again, then drew in a deep breath to calm herself. "I went from nothing to do, to way too busy."

"You can handle it," Reece said, returning to put the new order in the computer. She gave him the message from Brent as he tapped the screen, and he nodded acknowledgment. "Listen," he said, once the order was processing. "I'm sure you'll get the job—who wouldn't want you? But are they going to mind if you're moonlighting?"

"I'm sure I can make it work with them. They really seem to be interested in me. The interview was like something out of the Manual for Awesome Interviews."

"So what's the point of tonight?" Reece asked, his arms crossed as he studied her.

"Don't do that," Jen ordered. "Don't get all cynical on me."

He raised his hands. "Just asking a question."

She made a frustrated noise in the back of her throat. This was *so* Reece. "It makes perfect sense. They want to see how I perform under pressure. And I thrive in the hot seat, so I'm golden."

"What's the event?" Amanda asked, though Jenna couldn't tell if she was legitimately curious or trying to help shift the conversation.

"The company's been doing a campaign for a bridal company that centers around the selection of women for a wedding and bridesmaid calendar. The girls sent in their pictures, and tonight the winners are being announced. So they want all hands on deck. Like I said, it's the perfect time to see if I'm a pressure player."

"A wedding calendar?" Reece's brows rose.

"Just because you think marriage is a hideous trap that destroys love—"

"I'm pretty sure I said it was a ridiculous institution that sucks the lifeblood out of relationships and is doomed to failure. But the idea's the same."

Jenna rolled her eyes. She knew his views on marriage. She even understood them, to a degree. With a mother who'd walked out when Reece was fifteen, a father who'd remarried and divorced three more times and a best friend whose wife had packed her bags and skipped out on Brent and their newborn, it was no wonder Reece thought the institution of marriage was a crock. The last time one of their friends had gotten married, Reece had given them eight months.

They'd been divorced in six, and he'd practically oozed self-righteousness. "The only good marriages I've seen were Vincent's and Tyree's," he told her once. "And those ended in death."

Definitely a cynic. She, however, didn't share the sentiment. It was the lack of a marriage that had forced Jenna's own mom, Arlene, to struggle as a single mom, foolishly believing that Jenna's dad would see reason and return on a white horse, especially since he'd always told Arlene that he loved her and their daughter. He hadn't come back, of course, and Jenna had grown up with no sign of a father, except for four Christmas cards during her first five years, and with an over-worked mother.

But Arlene had finally married five years ago and was now blissfully happy in Florida with Jenna's stepfather. Which, as far as Jenna was concerned, disproved Reece's gloom-and-doom view of marriage.

"I think the idea of a bridal calendar is lovely," she said. "And from a marketing standpoint, it's very smart. Those girls will share with their friends, and then the calendars with the company logo will end up plastered on bedroom walls all over the city. Of course, if it were me, I would have done a contest. Had some sort of fashion show for sponsorship and then—"

She sat up straight, almost unable to believe she could be so incredibly brilliant.

"What?" Reece tilted his head, eyeing her. "You okay?"

"Jen?" Amanda leaned forward. "What is it?"

Jenna leaned back slowly, smiling so broadly her cheeks hurt. "Well, there you go," she said, eyeing Reece. "I've done it. I've just totally earned my way into this part-nership."

Chapter Nine

"CALENDAR GUYS?" Reece said, looking slightly baffled. "You want to do a calendar with a bunch of *guys?*"

"Yes!" Jenna hopped off her stool and started pacing, turning the idea over in her mind, searching for flaws—which she didn't find.

"Beefcake shots?" Amanda asked. "Like on romance novel covers?"

"You'd buy one, right?" Jenna asked, as Reece gaped at the two of them. "I mean look at him." She pointed to Reece. "Or Brent. Either one of them would look totally hot on a calendar."

She allowed herself only one moment to indulge in her memory of a shirtless Reece. All the times they'd gone to the pool or the beach. Lazy summer days where she'd read in the hammock at his dad's house while he and Brent did yard work. And of course, that drunken night in the shower eight months ago. The night she wasn't supposed to remember, but couldn't ever forget.

She bit back an indulgent sigh as Amanda squealed. "Are you kidding? I'd buy a dozen."

"See?" Jenna shot a smug look Reece's direction. "I've already earned my keep."

He, however, looked a little shell-shocked. "You want me to be on a calendar?"

"Well, you and Brent and ten others." She glanced around the bar. Surely ten of the guys would look equally hot shirtless? She met Amanda's eyes, and saw that her friend was thinking the exact same thing.

"I saw Tyree shirtless once," Amanda said. "I came to meet Brent here, and they were doing some work in the attic space. Ty came down to say hi. Poor guy was all hot and sweaty." She paused and sighed, probably reliving the moment. Then her mouth curved into a decadent smile. "Yeah," she said. "He'll do."

"Well, that's three," Jenna said. "Who else?" She turned to Reece. "I haven't been around for eight months. Who else is on payroll now who'd look hot on a calendar?"

"You're insane. I'm not stripping down for a calendar."

"I thought the whole idea was to help Tyree," she said, as he crossed his muscled arms over his chest. She scowled anew. "See, that pose would totally work."

"How is a picture of me and Brent and whoever else you drag kicking and screaming into this going to save the bar? We'd sell, what? A couple dozen? And all to the girl-friends of the guys who work here."

"Oh, you'd sell more than that," Amanda assured him. "Leave a stack by the door, or put a flyer in with the bill. People would buy."

"You mean *women* would buy."

"Well, duh." She took a sip of her Cosmo. Amanda had no qualms about drinking at lunch.

"The women would be coming in with men who'll buy them drink after drink in the hopes of taking his date home and getting laid." Jenna grinned. "Come on,

Reece. Even if you didn't work in a bar, you'd know the score."

He rolled his eyes. "Thanks for the assessment. I wasn't criticizing your marketing scheme, just pointing out the fact that ultimately the sale of calendars isn't going to get us where we need to be. Even with all those men buying drinks for their dates."

Jenna nodded. "You're right."

"Of course," Reece said, taking a bow as Amanda laughed.

Jenna ignored them both. She was too eager to make her point. "It needs to be bigger. We need to draw in people from the outside now, not wait until we have a calendar to sell. And who needs a calendar in April, anyway?"

Amanda and Reece exchanged looks, both clearly confused. "So you're not doing the calendar after all?" Amanda asked.

"Oh, we're doing it," Jenna assured them. "But it's not about the guys in the bar—"

"Thank goodness," Reece muttered.

"—it's a contest," Jenna concluded, shooting him a sideways look. "Contestants pulled from the outside *and* from the bar. You," she added with an innocent smile, "can be in the running for January."

"Now, wait a minute—"

He didn't get to finish the thought because Amanda's squeal was too loud. "I love that! You can do a contest every few weeks, promote the shit out of it, and that'll take you to—" She started to count on her fingers.

"October," Jenna said. "Just in time to get it printed for next year. It's brilliant, right? I mean, I'm not crazy?"

"Sweetie, you're a freaking genius."

"And we could add some of the recipes, too," Jenna

continued, on a roll. "Or, even better, we can do a calendar and then a companion cookbook, with pictures of the guys and some of the bar's bestselling drinks and recipes. Get it in local bookstores, maybe sell it nationally. That would be a great fundraiser. Don't you think?" she added, twisting around to look at Reece.

"You seriously think it'll work?"

"I know it will," she assured him, crossing her fingers out of sight. Because nothing in marketing was a certainty. She could organize the crap out of this thing, have the hottest guys under the sun, and the whole thing could still crash and burn.

But she was going to do her damnedest to make sure that didn't happen.

"Then I say we go for it," he said. "So long as I'm not one of your guinea pigs."

"Reece—"

"Not my style, babe. You know that. And I'm a partner now, remember? I'll have enough on my plate without preening for the masses."

"You don't have to preen," Jenna said. "Just strut." She managed to say it with a straight face, but couldn't hold back the giggles when he glared at her. "Fine," she said, holding up her hands. "Fine. You get a pass. *This* time. But I'm going all out on the marketing, and I expect you to be all in when I need you."

He looked her straight in the eye, his expression so intense it seemed to push her back in her chair. "Don't you know by now that I'll always be there when you need me?"

"I—" Her heart fluttered, and her skin flushed. And for the first time in ages, she couldn't hold eye contact with him. "Of course, I know that."

"Then you already know—whatever you need, all you have to do is ask."

"I—" She cut off her words, not certain what to say. There was something raw, almost dangerous, about the way he was looking at her. Like they were the only two people in the bar, and that he meant the words literally. Right then, she believed he'd throw himself off a building if she asked him to. And that, yes, he'd even do the contest. For her. If she asked.

He was giving her that power, and it humbled her so much that it was on the tip of her tongue to say something snarky and silly. The kind of thing she'd said to Reece-the-best-friend a million times. But those words wouldn't come for the Reece standing in front of her. They felt wrong. Off.

And so she said the only thing she could; she said, "Thank you."

"You're welcome," he said, his eyes staying right on hers, his voice so low and raw that it seemed to vibrate inside her. She swallowed, her hand closing around her Diet Coke, but she couldn't seem to conjure the will to lift it to her lips or to look away.

Beside her, Amanda cleared her throat. "Um, Reece?"

His head snapped to her, and the moment—or whatever the hell it was—evaporated like water on a hot Texas day.

Amanda cocked her head, indicating a couple who'd just settled onto two empty bar stools.

"Right." Reece glanced down the bar, saw that Eric was at the other end mixing drinks for a group of customers, and slid down to help the new people.

Immediately Amanda turned to Jenn, her eyes wide. "What was that?"

"What?" Jen asked, feigning ignorance.

"Don't even. For a second there, I thought I was going to have to tell you two to get a room."

"Oh, please." Jenna's face burned. "I don't know what you're talking about."

"Fine. I used to like playing make-believe, too. Then I grew up." She smiled and batted her eyes. "He wouldn't be a bad one to grow old with, I've got to say."

"Will you lower your voice?" Jenna shot an uneasy glance toward Reece. "And there isn't anything going on. He's one of my best friends."

"With benefits?"

"Dammit, Amanda, stop."

Amanda studied her for a second then took a thoughtful sip of her Cosmo before leaning back in her stool. "My mistake," she said. "Consider it dropped."

"Let's just focus on the project in front of me and not your overactive imagination, okay?"

Amanda lifted her hands in surrender. "You'll want to get the word out. Do you want me to talk to Nolan?"

"Would you? That would be great." Amanda's step-brother Nolan worked in radio, and although Jenna hadn't listened to his show since she moved back, she'd heard that he had a huge following for his comedic schtick mixed with local and classic tunes.

"No problem. And you'll need legal releases for the models. Probably the contestants, too. You'll want their pictures for promo, right?"

"Good point." She caught Reece's eye as he added a cherry to the drink he was making. "Who are we using for the partnership documents?"

His mouth curved into a frown. "Good question. We'll want someone other than Tyree's usual lawyer. Conflict of interest and all that." He glanced at Amanda. "You must work with attorneys all the time."

"Real estate, sure. But I can ask for a recommendation for y'all."

"Don't worry," Jenna said. "I'm going out with Easton tonight after the bridal event. I'll ask him if he can do it. Or if he can recommend someone."

"Easton?" Amanda's perfectly shaped brows rose. "How interesting."

Jenna laughed. "Hey, you tossed him aside."

She could feel Reece's eyes on her, and she made it a point not to turn toward him.

"I didn't exactly toss him, so much as the wind blew us in different directions. I just didn't realize you two had kept in touch."

"He called me a few months ago when he had depositions in LA. He was there for a week, and we went out a couple of times. He's a good guy."

"He's a great guy," Amanda agreed. Her lips curved into a wicked smile. "Yeah, I'd say great is a *very* accurate description."

"Amanda!" This time, Jenna didn't manage to check the instinct that had her glancing at Reece. He was squirting soda into a highball glass—and he overfilled the thing.

"Damn," he muttered, as she looked quickly away.

"It's just drinks and dessert," Jenna said, ostensibly to Amanda, but loud enough for Reece to hear. Which was stupid. Because why should he care who she went out with? And why should she care what he thought?

Except, of course, she knew the answer to that question. It just happened to be a question—and an answer—that she didn't want to ponder too deeply.

"At any rate," she said, her voice clipped and firm, "the point is that I can ask him about the partnership documents and the releases. And I want to ask him about nonmonetary compensation for work, too."

Both Reece and Amanda looked blank.

"Like if Maia agrees to help me out with some of the marketing work—I don't want to pay her cash since that defeats the purpose. But maybe a book of No Cover Charge coupons. Same goes for whatever carpenter we find to work on the stage."

"Oh, I may know somebody for that," Amanda said. "I know a guy who flips houses. In fact, I'm supposed to show him the Drysdale mansion again next week. That'll be the third time he's walked through it, and if he buys..." She trailed off with a whistle. "Well, that commission could keep me in chocolate and Cosmos for a long time, you know?"

"That's the huge mansion close to the Capitol building, right? The one that needs all the work."

"That's it." Amanda shrugged. "At any rate, if he's got the time, he might be interested in doing it."

"Yeah? And he's good?"

"Well, actually—"

Jenna rolled her eyes. "I mean his work, not his cock."

"Women," Reece muttered, but he looked amused.

"I don't know," Amanda said, looking prim. "Ours is a purely professional relationship."

"First time for everything," Jenna quipped, then ducked to avoid the balled-up napkin her friend tossed her way.

Reece shook his head in mock exasperation, then signaled to them that he'd be back soon before moving down to the far end of the long bar to go over something with Eric.

"But seriously," Amanda continued, "he used to have one of those remodeling shows on television. And every property he's worked on that I've sold for him has been top-notch. So he must have some idea what he's doing."

"He sounds like a real possibility," Jenna said. "You'll shoot me his info?"

"Of course. Although if he buys the mansion, he probably won't have time." She pursed her lips, considering. "Actually, I just thought of someone even better. My friend Brooke does commercial renovations, and she mentioned that she's looking for a high-profile project."

"Why? And what does that even mean?"

"Not a clue," Amanda admitted. "But I'll set up a meeting and you can figure it out. Call it my good deed for the day, even if you are a total bitch."

"Who's a bitch?" Reece's cousin, Mike, looking young and eager, staggered under two racks full of recently washed beer glasses. He plunked them down on the counter and started to put them away.

"According to Amanda, I am. But she loves me anyway. Which is why she's getting the check, right? My turn next, once I'm gainfully employed?"

"I already told you this one was on me," Amanda agreed. "You look familiar," she added to Mike. "Do I know you?"

"Reece's cousin," Jenna said. "I think y'all must have met somewhere, but who knows? You're a senior now, right?"

"Yup," Mike said. "Turned eighteen a few months ago, and I start at the University in the fall. Working as many hours as I can until then. Stocking up on cash, you know."

"Very responsible of you," Jenna said, as Amanda mouthed, *Too young. Too bad.*

Jenna rolled her eyes. Amanda liked to pretend she slept with anything that moved, but Jenna knew better. Her friend was more discriminating than that. But she never, ever got serious about a guy. Or, at least, she hadn't yet, despite Jenna's best efforts to pair Amanda with someone.

"Listen, I need to run," Jenna said. "I need to get all these ideas organized plus do some research for tonight."

"No prob," Amanda said. "Do you want me to drive you? Or are you going to call a ride share?"

"Oh, you don't have to do that," Mike said, squinting at a glass, and then polishing away some water spots.

"I don't?" Jenna looked to Amanda, who shrugged, just as confused. "Why don't I?"

"Because Reece got you a car." He was grinning ear to ear. "It's out back. He said you'd be surprised."

"He said he wanted to see the look on her face when she saw the surprise," Reece said, coming down the bar and smacking Mike with a hand towel. "Jerk."

"Sorry! I didn't want her running off to get an Uber or something."

"You seriously got me a car?" She couldn't take her eyes off Reece, standing there like a knight, his grin at least as bright as armor. "How could you afford that?"

"Didn't cost much," he said. "I made it for you. Or, rather, I restored it. Come on. It's parked in the loading zone out back."

Her heart hitched, and she tried to remember when, if ever, someone had done a thing like that for her. As far as she could recall, the answer was a big, fat never.

But there it was, a 1972 El Camino in a bright yellow. A classic cross between a truck and a car with a single bench seat in the front and a truck bed in the back. "Isn't that your grandfather's old car?"

"He bought himself a Lincoln. Said if I could get this one running again, I could have it. And since I knew you were coming back to Austin without a car..." He trailed off with a shrug. "It only took me a weekend. Well, once I got serious about fixing it up for you. I've been fiddling with it here and there during my days off."

She turned to him, her hand pressed over her heart.

"Reece." His name seemed to stick in her throat. "I can't believe you did this."

He reached for her hand, then squeezed lightly before pulling back, leaving the key ring behind. "Can't you?"

She lifted the keys, then fisted her hand around the metal, still warm from his touch. "Truthfully? I can. You got Mike a job. You're helping Tyree out. Of course, you got me a car." She cocked her head, looking at him. "I bet you're re-roofing your dad's place."

He chuckled. "No, just refinishing his kitchen cabinets."

She stepped forward, then rose up on tiptoes to brush a kiss over his cheek, his beard tickling her lips. "You're a good man, Reece Walker."

"Wait until you see how it drives before you go making assessments like that." He held the door open for her, and she got in, then rolled down the window once he closed the door. After a second, he cleared his throat. "Don't forget to talk to Easton about all the legal stuff. He can give me a call about the partnership documents."

"I won't forget." She slipped the key in the ignition but didn't start the car. He was still holding onto the window. "Um, anything else?"

"Huh? Oh, right." He lifted his hand away. "I was just wondering what you've got planned for Saturday."

"Oh." Her stomach did a little flip. "I don't know. Why?"

"The Fix is going to have a booth at Eeyore's Birthday Party. Brent and I were hoping you'd be coming, too. He's bringing Faith, of course."

"Oh," she repeated, as a thin sheen of disappointment settled over her. Which was ridiculous. She loved Eeyore's Birthday Party. The annual event at Pease Park was an Austin tradition, and she'd been going since she was a little girl. Plus, she loved Brent and Faith, and would happily work the bar's booth if they needed her. So what did she have to be disappointed about?

Absolutely nothing, she told herself firmly. Not one, single thing.

And with that, she turned the key, felt the engine rumble to life, and heard herself saying, "You know what? That sounds just about perfect for a Saturday."

EASTON WALLACE WAS A GODDAMN BASTARD.

That, at least, was Reece's current assessment of the man. Since Jenna had left, it had changed pretty much hourly—actually, a hell of a lot more frequently than that —and had ranged from *lucky s-o-b* to *conniving lady-killer who needed to be stopped.*

Not to mention every insult in between.

Which was probably a little unfair. After all, Reece had gone out with Easton for drinks a couple of times since that night at the Broken Spoke. And it was Reece himself who'd reminded Jenna to ask Easton about legal work.

What the hell had he been thinking?

Was he deliberately pushing her toward Easton? Toward any man other than himself?

Hell yeah, he was.

Why? Because Reece sucked at relationships, and Jenna deserved a good man.

And even if he didn't crash and burn every time he was with a woman, even if he didn't think that marriage was a convoluted ritual designed to kill passion and foment discontent, he still wouldn't pursue Jenna. Too much risk.

He'd much rather spend his life without her in his bed so long as it meant that she was in his life.

So why did he have the urge to bloody his fist against Easton's aristocratic nose?

Because the thought of Easton's hands—or, God forbid, his mouth—on Jenna was enough to make Reece—

"You okay?"

Reece spun around to find Brent leaning against the door frame of the small office where Reece had been pacing. "What?"

"You're prowling. You worried about all of this? Partnership? The plan?"

"Huh?" Reece shook his head, trying to shift gears. "What? No. No, not at all. I'm just thinking about Jenna."

Fuck. He hadn't meant to say that.

"I mean her job interview," he continued before Brent interrogated him. "This trial by fire tonight." He glanced at his watch. Past nine. "Guess we'll be hearing soon how it went."

"I bet she nailed it. You know Jenna. Whatever she puts her mind to..."

"Yeah, you're right. I'm just—doesn't matter. I'm going to go relieve Cameron." Reece pushed past Brent, feeling like he'd dodged a bullet, then headed toward the back bar and tapped Cam on the shoulder. "Go take your dinner break. I'll cover for you."

"Yeah?" Cam's brow furrowed, probably because Reece usually didn't cover for the employees when they were well-staffed. Today, however, Reece wanted the distraction of mixing drinks—because if he was thinking about the pour, that meant he wasn't thinking about Jenna.

He spent the next hour pouring drinks, circulating among the customers, chatting up the regulars, and generally keeping his mind on the work—and absolutely nothing else.

He'd mostly succeeded in pushing thoughts of Jenna

behind a mental curtain when the vibration of his phone in his hip pocket startled him. He snatched it out, glanced at the screen, and everything he'd been fighting against fell away.

It was Jenna.

He answered on the second ring. "Hey, how'd the interview go? Do you know—"

"Reece?" Her voice cracked.

"Jenna?"

He heard a gulp, then a gasp. Then her words came, tight and strangled. "Can you hear me?"

Christ, was she crying? "Hey, hey, calm down." He kept his voice low and soothing, the way he did when he was sitting with Faith, and she woke up from a nightmare. Inside, though, his heart was pounding. "Are you okay?" Images of car wrecks filled his mind. Or lanky, muscled teens with iron pipes in their hands and anger on their faces. "Can you tell me what's going on?"

"I just—I just—" Her voice broke, and he heard her draw in a loud breath, obviously trying to pull herself together. "I'm sorry," she finally managed. "I know you're working. But can you come? Please, Reece. I need you to come."

Chapter Ten

JENNA PACED the length of the car and back again, her feet moving because if she stopped, she'd cry or scream or throw herself into the bed of the El Camino and cry like a baby.

Dammit. How could she have been so stupid? So ridiculously naive?

And where was Reece? He should be here by now. She wasn't more than fifteen minutes from downtown, and she'd called at least twenty minutes ago. But he still hadn't come, and the more the minutes ticked by, the stupider she felt for ringing him in the first place. She should have called Brent. Or Amanda. Or, hell, she could have called Easton.

But her fingers had dialed Reece, and now he was going to see her like this, worn down, defeated, and a sniveling, mascara-lined mess.

Where was he?

She wiped her eyes again as the squeal of tires echoed in the distance, followed by headlights cresting the small hill that led to the parking lot she was currently pacing.

And then Blue pulled up, and Reece was sprinting from the truck to her side.

"Jenna." His hands clasped her upper arms, and he held her in place as he examined her, his eyes taking in every inch of her, his inspection so meticulous that she knew he must be seeing her disappointment, her embarrassment, her frustration.

Her fear.

Not of the dark. Not of the dangers of being stranded in a dark and secluded parking lot.

No, this fear was new, and it stemmed from the wildness she saw in his expression. A fire so intense it could reduce her to ashes. And she saw something else, too. A promise. Or maybe a threat.

She wasn't sure. But as he bent toward her, she felt her breath catch in her throat and her chest tighten in anticipation. *He was going to kiss her.*

She drew in a sharp breath, and the sound acted as a talisman, breaking the spell. He froze, his posture shifting almost imperceptibly, but enough for Jenna to know that the possibility of a kiss had faded with that errant breath— and she wasn't sure if she should be relieved or very, very disappointed.

"God, Jenna, you scared the hell out of me. Are you okay?"

He pulled her close, crushing her against his chest. And at that moment, she realized just how worried he'd been—and how desperately she'd needed to see him tonight.

His fingers dug into her arms as he eased her back away from him. This time, his eyes fixed on hers. He released his grip, then brushed her hair back from her face, the gesture so tender she wrapped her arms around his waist and hugged him close.

"I'm okay," she whispered, her voice muffled against his chest. "I'm okay now."

"What happened? Are you hurt? Did someone—"

"No. Nothing like that." She swallowed, gathering herself, then stepped back. Her emotions had been all over the place—*she'd* been all over the place. But now that he was here, she felt calmer. And all the more foolish because of it.

"I—it's not as bad as you'd think from looking at me. Promise. It's just, I don't know. Everything piled up on top of everything else. I mean, I'd thought they were serious about me getting this job, but then—"

"You didn't get it?"

"Not even close," she said. "The whole situation was a crock. It was me and a half-dozen other candidates, and it was so damn obvious that they weren't legitimately interested in any of us. We were just there to be cost-free labor, and—" She clenched her fists at her side, because she didn't want to think about it anymore. For over an hour now, she'd been kicking herself for being so stupid. For getting her hopes up about something that had seemed like the perfect situation, but the truth was she should have seen the warning signs.

"I'm sorry," he said gently, pulling her back into his embrace. He stroked her back, his hand going in small circles, and she smiled against his shoulder, feeling soothed and safe.

"I just feel so stupid."

"You thought you'd found exactly what you were looking for. And you were too close—and too excited—to see the dark underbelly."

She closed her eyes and nodded against his chest. "Thanks for coming."

"Are you kidding me? I'll always be here for you."

"I didn't even tell them I was leaving." She gestured back toward the warehouse inside which the company was filming. "I just ran out. All I could think about was getting away from here, but then the car wouldn't start, and—"

Tears clogged her throat, and he cupped her chin, looking deep into her eyes. "Hey, none of that. I'm here now. The power of three, remember?" He raised his hand, and she met him with a fist bump the way the three of them had all through high school.

"But only two tonight," she said. "You didn't bring Brent."

"Yeah, well, you didn't call him."

She felt her cheeks heat and hoped he didn't notice. The only one she'd wanted was Reece.

She didn't tell him that, though. Instead, she lifted a shoulder, looked down at the pavement, and said, "Well, you know. I figured you're the one who can fix the car." She lifted her head to look at him. "You can, right?"

"I'll give it a whirl."

She stepped back, giving him room to deal with the car. He popped the hood, then handed her his phone so she could aim the light at the engine. She had no idea what he was doing, but he pulled a small army knife out of his pocket, then fiddled with something, then tweaked something else.

After a few minutes of that, he stepped free of the hood and stood up to look at her. "That should do it."

"Thank you." She swallowed. "I'm—well, I'm meeting Easton in half an hour, and I don't want to be late."

His jaw tightened. "No. Definitely wouldn't want that."

For a moment, they just looked at each other. Then she wiped her palms on her skirt and cleared her throat. "Well. Anyway. I, um, guess I'll see if it starts now."

She took a step toward the driver's door. She didn't

make it. Instead, Reece's hand closed around her wrist, and he pulled her back, his arm looping around her waist as his mouth crushed hard against hers. Immediately, she melted, her body going warm and soft and pliable even as she felt him harden against her. She moaned, the sound coming unbidden, and he took advantage, his tongue sweeping inside her mouth. Taking. Tasting.

Demanding.

Something inside her cried out that she should be retreating. That this was a mistake, and she needed to push him away. To back off.

But she didn't. She *couldn't*. Because this was Reece. This was what—*who*—she wanted.

And so she did the only thing she could do.

She surrendered.

REECE HAD IMAGINED this moment hundreds—no, thousands—of times over the last eight months. The heat of her in his arms. The taste of her mouth. The pressure of her lips against his.

He'd spent long hours imagining the pressure of her body against his, her skin hot, her pulse rapid with desire.

Again and again, he'd succumbed to the fantasy of this wild, perfect moment.

And yet his imagination had never come close to the reality of the woman he now held in his arms.

Still, though, it wasn't enough. He craved her. Needed her.

Inside him, a dam had burst, and all of the desire he'd been fighting was spilling out, threatening to steal his reason and overwhelm his senses.

His mouth warred with hers, taking and teasing, the

kisses so wild and rough that he tasted blood. His cock ached, and with every low, passionate noise she made he felt himself grow harder, until all he could think about was tossing her into the back of the El Camino and burying himself inside her as the stars shone down on them.

He wanted to feel her yield to him, to lose himself in her heat. He wanted to kiss every inch of her body. To memorize the texture of her skin and explore every crevice, every curve.

Hell, he wanted her at his mercy, and the knowledge that she wanted him too both humbled and amazed him.

"Jenna," he murmured, because he had to feel her name on his lips. Then he thrust his fingers into her hair and held her head steady so he could claim her mouth once more.

He used his other hand to explore her body, relishing the small sounds of arousal as he cupped her ass through her skirt. He wanted to pull the material up and slide his hand between her legs, then explore her slick, wet folds.

His cock twitched at the thought, but he forced his hand the other direction. Soon enough he'd lose himself in that sweet heat. Right now, the temptation was too great, and as much as the thought aroused him, he had no intention of fucking Jenna in the back of the El Camino.

Not tonight, anyway.

Instead, he moved his hand over her hip, along the curve of her waist, then higher until his fingers brushed the swell of her breast. He felt a shiver run through her, then heard her whisper his name.

"Jenna," he murmured as he cupped his hand over her breast, his thumb stroking her nipple, hard now under the thin material of her bra and her blouse.

She drew in a shuddering breath, her back arching in an invitation to a more intimate touch.

He wanted to accept. Hell, he wanted to rip the blouse wide open, to tug her bra down and flick his tongue over her nipple until she cried out for more.

And she would—he knew she would.

She was his now. No more waiting. No more wishing.

His.

Dear God, she was finally his.

And he intended to take his time to explore every inch of her, punishing her with unrelenting pleasure until she screamed his name and begged him to please, please take her, and—

"—*please...*"

The word, so recently at the center of his fantasy, caught his attention. "Jenna, we—"

"—can't," she finished, pulling away from him. She stood there, breathing hard, her expression miserable. "Reece, I'm sorry. I'm so, so sorry. But this is—I mean, it's not. I mean, we can't—"

She cut herself off again, then bit her lower lip before swallowing hard and tilting her head up to meet his eyes. "Don't hate me," she whispered, "but I just can't."

Chapter Eleven

REECE OPENED the bottle of Jack he kept in the cabinet beside his sink, poured himself a shot, then hurled the damn glass across the room without even taking a sip.

Fuck.

He'd lost her.

She'd been right there. *His.* Right in his arms, exactly where she was supposed to be. And somehow he'd fucking lost her.

He dropped down onto the sofa, then took a swig straight from the bottle, closing his eyes as the whiskey burned its way down the back of his throat.

Why the hell should he be surprised? He knew damn well that even if he had her, he'd never be able to keep her. Each and every one of his relationships had fallen apart. He just hadn't expected the end with Jenna to come only minutes after the beginning.

With a groan, he let his head fall back while he rubbed his chest in a futile effort to heal the jagged wound she'd inflicted when she'd ripped herself away from him so that she'd be on time for Easton.

Fucking Easton, a goddamn pretty boy attorney. One who didn't live in an apartment over his father's garage. Who was steady. Interesting. And who hadn't gambled away his life's savings to help a friend.

Hell, he was probably good for her. And, God knew, Jenna deserved the best.

So, no, Reece didn't begrudge the man. Even if he did want to kill him.

He took another swallow and sighed as the liquid fire lit his veins. It had been one hell of a crappy night. And the worst of it? That the one person he wanted to talk to was the one person he couldn't call. *Fuck.*

He couldn't even ring Brent. For one thing, Reece had no interest in confessing the truth. For another, he happened to know that Brent was still at The Fix. He was on until closing, and after that, he was crashing, planning to grab a few hours of sleep before spending his day off tomorrow with Faith. A school day, but considering Faith was still in kindergarten, he'd told Reece that he was willing to break the rules.

Maybe he should call Megan...

She might not be able to burn the thought of Jenna out of his mind completely, but she could at least give him a few hours peace.

He started to reach for his phone, then pulled his hand back. It wasn't peace he wanted; not really. He'd rather feel this way and crave Jenna than have another woman in his bed. Because no matter how much he might like the woman or how good the sex might be, it couldn't be anything but hollow.

And Reece didn't think he could ever settle for hollow again.

Frustrated, he took another sip, then closed his eyes and tilted his head back. He didn't intend to go to sleep, but the next thing he knew the light from his east-facing window was streaming in, warming his skin and urging his eyes to open and face a new day.

A day without Jenna.

The thought made him groan, and he forced himself off the couch. His muscles protested—he'd slept all night sprawled half-on and half-off his sofa—and his head ached with the dull throbbing of a hangover and the uncomfortable residue of Jenna-filled dreams. He felt like shit, but he was determined not to spend the day watching a mental movie of Jenna rolling around in bed with Easton.

By seven, he'd shoved a faded concert T-shirt over his head and had tugged on a pair of threadbare jeans. By seven-fifteen, he'd washed down a piece of toast with a glass of orange juice. And by seven-thirty he was under the carport, a power sander rumbling in his hand as he stripped a layer of cracked, faded varnish off the final door of his dad's kitchen cabinets.

He worked slowly, meticulously, letting the work beat back all other thoughts until there was nothing but him and the wood and the promise of turning something old and battered into something shining and new. Soon enough, he made the final pass, then switched off the machine and turned around to find a tack cloth.

It wasn't hard to find. As soon as he reached out, his father put the grungy brown cloth into his hand. "Little early for carpentry, isn't it, son?"

"Oh, hell, Dad. Sorry. Did I wake you?"

His dad waved the question away. "You know me. I'm up with the sun. And Edie's never slept past six in her life. But I haven't seen you up this early since, oh, never."

Reece smirked. He'd never been an early riser, but his father was also prone to exaggeration. "Just trying to make some progress." He'd taken on the cabinet project a few weeks ago after his dad's current girlfriend, Edie, had made an offhand remark about how battered they were looking. Reece figured he'd do the kitchen cabinets first, then tackle the bathrooms in the summer.

"I saw you come in," his father said, leaning against one of the carport's support posts, then lighting a cigarette.

"Those things will kill you," Reece said automatically. He'd been trying to get his dad to quit for his entire life, with no luck. For that matter, his dad's three ex-wives—including Reece's mother—had been equally unpersuasive.

"Might do," his dad said, just as he always did. His father had been smoking since he was fifteen years old, and had told them all that he didn't see any reason to quit now. "Was pretty late," he added, and it took Reece a second to realize they were back to talking about what time Reece got home last night.

"Well, what with being thirty and all, I thought I could stay out without calling home first."

"Stayed up pretty late, too," his dad continued, clearly ignoring the sarcasm. "Saw your light on," he added, by way of explanation. "Now here you are, up with the sun."

"Your point?"

His dad exhaled a cloud of smoke. "Just wondering if there's something on your mind."

Reece sighed. He should have known it was coming. "No," he lied. "Okay, yes. I was thinking I might want to stay in the apartment a little bit longer than I'd originally planned. I'm not quite ready to dive into building the house yet, and so long as you don't mind me living in your backyard, I'd rather not deal with the hassle of moving all my stuff."

The lie rolled out easily. The last thing Reece wanted to do was tell his miserly father that he'd essentially given his savings to Tyree in exchange for part ownership in a failing bar.

Not that Reece was pessimistic about their chances—he wasn't. He just didn't want a lecture from his father. Reece might be thirty years old and able to bench press over two hundred and fifty pounds, but as far as Charlie Walker was concerned, Reece was still the skinny fourth-grader getting picked on by the sixth-grade bully.

"Should be okay," Charlie said. "Edie was thinking about letting young Oliver stay there starting in late August."

"Oliver?"

"Her youngest grandbaby. Starting at UT in the fall. You figure you'll still be in the apartment then?"

Reece raised a brow. "You figure you'll still be with Edie?"

"Don't be impertinent, boy. You think I don't know what a good thing I have with that woman?"

"I think you go through women like some men go through handkerchiefs."

His dad made a rough noise in the back of his throat. "If you need a place, the apartment's yours. Anything else you want to talk about?"

"Not a thing."

His father stubbed out his cigarette, then gave him a long, thoughtful look.

"Something else on your mind?" Reece asked.

"You're a good man."

A frown tugged at Reece's mouth as he glanced toward the cabinets. "What? These? I should have been finished by now."

"The cabinets. Fixing up that apartment even though it's not going to be yours forever. The truck."

"Truck?"

"Your granddad's old El Camino. I heard you gave it to Jenna."

"She's tight right now," Reece said, his senses sharpening at the mention of her.

"Not criticizing. That girl's like family."

"Right." Reece shoved his hands into his pockets. "Anything else?"

"Talked to Tyree last night."

"Oh?"

"He told me about the partnership." His dad's voice had softened, and although it might have been Reece's imagination, he thought he heard a hint of pride. "The apartment's yours for as long as you need it."

A lump formed in Reece's throat, and he swallowed it down. "What about Edie's grandson?" he asked, reaching for a fresh tack cloth.

"Phfft. Dorms are good for a kid. And don't worry about getting your house."

Reece looked up sharply, surprised. The straightforward acknowledgment of what Reece had done for Tyree—and what he'd given up in the process—was uncharacteristic for Charlie.

"If it's your dream, you'll make it. Sometimes dreams take a while," Charlie added. "Hell, sometimes you don't even know what your dream is until it's staring you in the face."

An unfamiliar twinkle danced in his father's eyes. "Dad?"

But Charlie just waved the words away. "Don't mind me. I'm just an old man rambling. Bottom line is that I'm proud of you, son." He pushed away from the post, standing up straight. "Now Edie and I are off to breakfast, then we've got an appointment with a travel agent."

"A travel agent? Dad, I keep telling you that it's simple

to book flights on the Internet. You don't have to go through an agent."

"We're thinking about taking a cruise. Figure we should do it right."

The back door opened, and Edie stepped out, her gray hair teased high. Born and bred in the Panhandle, Edie still embraced the stereotypical big Texas hair.

"Look at you," she said, coming over to give Reece a hug, which he easily returned, breathing in the scent of Shalimar perfume and Pond's face cream. "I'm going to fix you the biggest breakfast ever once all those cabinets are back in. You're just the sweetest boy."

"I'll take it," Reece said. Of all the women who'd come in and out of his father's life, Edie was the one he'd miss the most when it ended.

Because with his dad, it always ended.

Like father like son, he thought, watching as Charlie opened the Cadillac's passenger door for Edie.

And as Charlie backed the car out of the drive, Reece kept on thinking. About how many women had crossed his own bed. And about the fact that he hadn't truly wanted any of them. Not permanently, anyway. They were transient comfort. Companions for a while, but not for forever.

He'd never found a forever woman.

Or maybe he had, and he was just too afraid of upsetting the status quo to do something about it.

Sometimes you don't even know what your dream is until it's staring you in the face.

His father's words echoed in his head, and he had to give the old man props. Because he was right. Goddammit, he was right.

Jenna.

She'd been in front of him for his entire damn life, but

he'd been too blind to realize it until that night before she left for LA. The night that everything flipped.

And instead of accepting the truth and doing something about it, he'd been fighting reality ever since.

Or he had been. Last night, he'd stopped fighting. Last night, he'd pulled her close and claimed her. And, dammit, it had felt right. Perfect, even.

At least until she'd pulled away.

But he'd seen the truth in her eyes and felt it in her kisses. She wanted him, too; he was certain of it.

And now Reece knew what he had to do.

For years, he'd been fighting his own desire, but he was done with that.

Now, he had a new battle to wage.

Now, he had to fight for Jenna.

Chapter Twelve

EXCEPT for a few office buildings that stood at the corner of Sixth and Congress, the blocks of Sixth Street that extended between Congress Avenue and Interstate 35 were occupied primarily by restaurants and bars. Which meant that the street had a stale, abandoned feel at eight in the morning.

Not that Jenna minded. She was feeling rather stale and abandoned herself. And since she'd barely slept at all last night, she thought she'd come into The Fix early, plunk herself down at one of the battered desks in the office, and start organizing her lists.

She'd parked a few blocks down in one of the all-day lots and was half a block away when she heard someone call her name. She stopped, then turned back to look over her shoulder and found Megan hurrying toward her, pulling a large rolling case.

"Hey, good to see you again," Jenna said. "Where are you off to this early?"

"One of the local magazines is putting together a story

about the Capitol staff. I'm doing make-up for the clerks and staffers they picked for the photo shoot."

"Walking?"

Megan waved away the question. "It's just a few blocks, and I'm used to dragging this thing around. It's more make-up than I need, but it makes the clients feel like they're getting their money's worth."

Jenna smiled. She liked Megan, even if she was sleeping with Reece.

The thought came unbidden, and Jenna cringed. Because it was hardly her business who Reece slept with.

"Everything okay?" Megan asked.

"Oh, just something in my shoe."

"Here." She rolled the cart to Jenna. "It's sturdy. Sit and take it out."

"Oh, it's nothing." But Megan already had the cart there, and Jenna already felt foolish. She sat, lifted her foot, and took off her ballet flat. "There," she lied as she stood up again. "I think I got it. Thanks."

"No problem," Megan said, shifting the cart so she could continue rolling it westward down the street.

They fell into step together, silent at first, and then Megan cleared her throat. "Listen, I just want you to know that the thing between Reece and me—it wasn't serious."

Jenna stopped. "It wasn't?"

"No. We just—a good time, you know." Her cheeks flushed, but she looked Jenna in the eye as she spoke.

Jenna frowned. "Um, why are you telling me this?"

"Oh. Well. I thought—aren't you and Reece involved?"

Jenna's eyes widened. "Oh, no. No!" She thought of last night's crazy, foolish kiss, felt her entire body flush, and stressed the last part again. "No, no. We're just good friends."

"Oh!" Megan shook her head. "I'm sorry. He'd told me

you weren't. But he'd been so distracted by the fact that he hadn't picked you up, and then when I saw the way he looked at you in the bar, I thought—well, never mind."

"What?"

"Well, obviously it was my imagination."

"Totally," Jenna said emphatically. "Absolutely your imagination." Inside, though, something warm and pleasant and a little disturbing began to flow through her veins. "But how funny that you thought so," she added, her voice sounding odd even to her ears.

They'd reached The Fix, and Jenna enjoyed a wash of relief. She was completely out of ideas as to where to take the conversation next. "This is my stop. Have fun on your shoot."

"Thanks. Maybe I'll come by later."

"Great." Jenna's smile was so broad her cheeks ached. "I'll tell Reece you said hi," she added, then waited until Megan had crossed the street before closing her eyes and mentally kicking her own ass. Honestly, what the hell had she been doing? She had no interest whatsoever in seeing Megan and Reece get together.

Which was ridiculously bitchy and selfish of her, because she had no intention of keeping him for herself, either.

Escaping inside the empty bar was a relief, and soon Jenna was settled behind one of the desks in the office with a pad of paper in front of her, a *The Fix on Sixth* pen in her hand, and her mind whirring with tasks and plans.

And thoughts of Reece.

An hour later, she'd managed to accomplish exactly nothing, despite a billion things that needed to happen to get the calendar contest underway, a hundred phone calls she needed to make if she was going to pull together a solid marketing plan, and on and on and on.

There were proposals to write, vendors to retain, printers to line up, media to contact. So much that had to be done, and yet all she had to show for her efforts was a notepad covered with doodles.

Fuck.

Tears pricked her eyes as she ripped the page of useless scribbles off her notepad. Nothing was working out. Not the calendar contest she was trying to organize. Not her search for a new job. And definitely not this morning's plan to focus on The Fix and get her mind off Reece.

Damn the man. He'd ruined everything.

Okay, maybe not everything. He did rescue her from a dark parking lot in an unfamiliar section of South Austin. But then he'd kissed her, and now there was this thing between them. And the whole situation was an awkward, horrible mess.

Well, maybe not the *whole* situation. The kiss had been incredible. But the rest of it was horrible. Confusing and uncomfortable. Because she and Reece and Brent had always been a threesome. A perfect platonic triangle.

At least, that's what she'd been telling herself ever since she moved back to Austin.

Telling herself? Try *lying* to herself.

She should have put a stop to it right away. If she was any kind of woman—any kind of *friend*—she should have shoved hard against his chest the moment his lips met hers. She should have pushed him firmly away and told him that there was nothing but friendship between them.

But she hadn't.

God help her, she'd kissed him back. And even now, she could feel the echo of that kiss reverberating through her soul, hot and deep and wild and brutal.

It had burned inside her, melting her will and firing her senses. And it had taken all of her strength to finally break that kiss when what she'd really wanted was to beg him to bend her over the hood of the car, yank down her panties, and take her right there under the light of moon.

"You're an idiot, Jen," she whispered to herself. "A Grade-A, one-hundred-percent, award-winning idiot."

"Maybe," a deep voice said from the doorway. "But you're an adorable one."

Reece.

She kept her head down, certain her cheeks were flushed. God knew the rest of her was. The sound of his voice alone had made her skin go hot and her nipples peak. And there was a dangerous throbbing between her thighs.

Best not to lift her head. She'd just keep working, and he'd go away. He was a smart man, after all. Surely, he'd get the hint.

"Jenna." His voice was firm. Commanding. And it cut through her like an electric current leading to all her most private parts. "Dammit, Jenna, look at me."

She obeyed, tilting her chin as she raised her eyes, then inhaled sharply at the sight of him leaning against the doorjamb. The faded jeans that hung low on his hips. His muscles that strained under a vintage Jethro Tull T-shirt. The shirt hid most of his ink, but the art on his ripped biceps and forearms was on full display. Two vibrant sleeves of intertwined leaves, petals, and waves that not only drew her attention but also reminded her of the way he'd held her last night. The strength as he'd pulled her close. The confidence as he'd kissed her hard.

The memory washed over her once again, sparking a wild, liquid heat that burned through her, making her a little crazy. And very, very needy.

Oh, crap.

She looked down again, took a deep breath to steady

herself, then lifted her eyes to his face. "You shouldn't be here."

He stepped all the way into the office, then closed the door behind him. And, she noticed, he locked it. "We need to talk."

She made a scoffing sound as she pushed out of her chair and stalked around the desk. "Talk? Maybe you should have thought of that before you accosted me in the parking lot."

"Accosted?" The corner of his mouth rose just slightly. "Is that what I did? I could have sworn it was a rescue."

"You're *smiling*?" She heard the edge in her voice and was glad about it. She welcomed irritation, even anger. Anything to stifle the burning need that had begun to pulse between her thighs.

"You think this is funny?" She took another step toward him. "Do you know what you've done? What you've destroyed? You and me and Brent—"

"*No.*" The word lashed out, as hard as steel. "We three are together for a lot of things," he said softly. "But Brent's not any part of this."

He'd moved closer as he spoke, and now he was right in front of her, so close she could see the pulse beating in his neck.

"And just what is *this*?" she snapped.

His eyes narrowed, and for a moment she thought he was going to ignore the question. But then his gaze raked over her, the quick inspection somehow more possessive than last night's kiss had been. "I guess that depends on you."

His words surprised her. Considering the nature of that heated glance, she'd almost expected him to take her by the hair and drag her to him caveman style. And it flustered her to realize that part of her truly wanted that. In theory, if not in actual practice.

Confused and frustrated, she shook her head, trying to clear it. "We can't—"

"Why?" He stepped closer, then crooked his finger under her chin, forcing her to look up at him. "Does Brent want you, too? I thought you told me that was all in my imagination."

"It was. It is." Her voice was thick. Husky. And right then the only thing she knew in the whole world was the pressure of his finger burning against her skin. "Reece, please. You can't—"

"Or maybe it's Easton? Is he my competition?"

"I—"

He pressed a finger to her lips, silencing her. "If so, then why aren't you still in his bed? Why are you here, alone, thinking of last night with me instead of the rest of the night with him?"

She swallowed. "What makes you so sure I was thinking of you?"

He didn't even bother to answer. Why should he? He knew her well enough to know that he was right. "Tell me," Reece demanded as he trailed his finger along the neckline of the white T-shirt she'd paired with a slim black skirt. "Why aren't you with Easton?"

His fingers brushed the swell of her breast. "Why isn't he touching you? Claiming you?"

She gasped as his fingers gripped the cup of her bra and tugged it down, forcing her breast to pop free of both the bra and her shirt. "Reece!" she cried, but he squeezed her nipple between his fingers, and his name came out strangled, lost inside her breathy gasp of decadent pleasure.

"Why?" The word was as forceful as the way he

grasped her waist and pulled her toward him, and the pressure of her body against his sent electric shocks of bone-deep longing racing through her veins.

"Why isn't he kissing you?" Reece growled, his thumb leaving her breast to stroke roughly over her lower lip. He pressed his hips forward, and she could feel the outline of his erection against her belly. "Why isn't he taking what's his?"

"Why aren't you?" The words came out as a strangled whisper, and she knew she was playing with fire. "You're not kissing me." She reached around him and cupped his ass with her palms, increasing the pressure of his cock against her. "You're not fucking me, either. You're not doing anything except teasing me."

She felt more than heard his low groan. It vibrated through him, a potent mix of pleasure and torment that culminated in a violent passion when his mouth closed roughly over hers, claiming her just as he said he would.

Just as she'd wanted him to, damn her.

The kiss was hot and hard, and she opened her mouth to his, losing herself to the taste of him. The sweep of his tongue as he explored her mouth. The nip of his teeth against her lips. This wasn't a kiss, it was a substitute for sex, and every cell in her body knew it. Her skin felt warm, her nipples hard as stones. And the ache between her thighs was so intense that it took a monumental effort to keep from straddling his leg and rubbing herself shamelessly against him simply to relieve the pressure.

He shifted his stance, stepping back and breaking the contact between them. She whimpered in protest, but soon his hands were on her hips, and he was slowly gathering up her skirt. She held her breath as slowly—so deliciously, painfully slowly—he revealed her bare thighs.

"Reece..."

"Hush," he ordered. "Take a step back."

She swallowed, but silently complied, then found herself trapped between the man and the desk.

"Lift your skirt," he demanded as her heart pounded in her chest. "All the way up to your waist. I want to see your panties."

"Maybe I'm not wearing any," she teased.

He chuckled, the sound low in his throat. "That's okay, too. But I hope you are. Plain white cotton. Bikini style. Crisp and bright against the brown of your tan."

"It's April." Her mouth was dry, and she swallowed. "I'm not very tan. And what makes you think that's what I'm wearing?"

"Not thinking," he said. "Hoping." His hands were on her legs, his thumbs positioned to stroke her soft inner thigh. A feather-light touch that was sending an electrical current up her thighs to pool at her core.

"Why?" She whispered the word, her eyes closed as her sex burned, throbbing with a violent need to be touched. To be taken.

"We were in ninth grade, and we were in the courtyard of your apartment complex, and Brent had snuck a bottle of his dad's bourbon into his backpack before he came over. Do you remember?"

She tilted her head, trying to conjure the memory. "We'd just finished final exams before Christmas break, and my mom was working late. So we were celebrating. And I'd never had bourbon before."

"Brent told you that you needed to learn to drink like a guy if you were going to hang with us."

"And I said that I could put away as much bourbon as either of you and still be a girl. Oh, my," she added. "I'd forgotten."

"I'm not surprised. You weighed about half of what Brent or I weighed, but you matched us drink for drink."

"Took me until my last year in college before I could stomach bourbon again."

"Not me," Reece said. "I think I loved it all the more after that night."

A slow warmth rose up Jenna's neck. "I'm scared to ask why," she admitted.

"You seriously don't know?"

She closed her eyes, trying to think back, but she had to shake her head. "I remember the drinking. And I remember telling my mom the next morning that we must have gotten some bad Tex-Mex at the dive at the end of the block. The rest is missing."

"Too bad we didn't have camera phones back then," he said. "I would have cherished those photos."

"Tell me," she demanded, laughing as she gave his shoulder a shove.

"Like I said, you matched us drink for drink. But then you got it into your head that you had to prove that you were a girl. So you stripped off your jeans and T-shirt and dove into the water."

"I got into the pool? In the winter? Why?"

He shook his head, obviously fighting laughter. "I have no idea. But thank God you didn't drown, because Brent and I were so gobsmacked we just stood there laughing our asses off. Or, at least, we laughed until you climbed out."

Her entire body flushed. "White cotton panties and a matching cotton bra. That's about all I wore in high school."

"I could see your nipples—hard and tight from the cold water. And the dark shadow of your pubic hair against the wet panties."

"Oh." Her breath stuttered in her throat. "Did it make you hard?"

"Hell, yes. I told myself you were my best friend. That you were just being a goof. That I couldn't possibly want you."

"But you did." She lifted the skirt a tiny bit higher, revealing more thigh, but not yet showing her panties. "You did want me."

He dropped to his knees in front of her, then tilted his head back to meet her eyes. "Hell, yes," he said. "I pushed it away. Buried it. Ignored it. But I never stopped."

"White cotton," she confirmed, her heart pounding so hard she feared she'd crack a rib. "But you won't see any pubic hair, not even if they're wet. I'm waxed."

"Oh, baby. Show me."

It was an order she couldn't disobey, and she tugged her skirt the rest of the way up, exposing the plain cotton panties that she would never think were boring again.

"That's my girl," he said, his fingertip tracing the elastic of the leg hole, the sensation so deliciously erotic that she had to reach back and grasp the edge of the desk just to keep her knees from buckling.

"And what do you know?" he murmured as his fingertip slipped inside her panties. "You *are* wet."

"Very," she said. "Reece, please."

"Please what?"

"You know."

"Do I?" His finger slid over her folds, the tip dipping inside her in slow, methodical thrusts.

She closed her eyes and tilted her head back. "Oh, God."

"Is this what you want?"

"More," she murmured. "Please."

"Tell me," he said. "I want to hear you say it."

She licked her lips. She wanted to beg for his cock. She wanted him inside her so much her pussy was clenching in anticipation. And she knew he wanted it, too. But some ridiculous, unreasonable fear was telling her not to say it out loud. That as soon as she did, all of this would disappear, and she'd be left frustrated and embarrassed because she'd reached for more than she deserved.

"Please," she said. "Don't make me."

He pulled back, and her head snapped down, afraid that he'd stopped for good. She saw his furrowed brow, and she knew he was puzzled by her. She tried to think what to say, but he saved her from the effort when he took the finger he'd been touching her with and lifted it to her mouth. Gently, he stroked her lower lip until she drew the digit in and sucked, her head spinning from her own musky taste mingled with the sweetness of his skin.

"It's okay, baby," he finally said. "There's nothing to be scared of. It's me. It's you, and it's me."

Slowly, he withdrew the finger, then put his hands around her waist and lifted her to the desk. "Spread your legs and let me prove it to you."

She did as ordered, spreading her legs wide, and then putting her hands behind her to balance when he tugged her right to the edge of the desk. He dropped back to his knees, then trailed kisses up her inner thigh until he reached the apex.

Slowly—so wonderfully slowly—he traced the tip of his tongue along the edge of her panties before closing his mouth over her pussy. He sucked and bit through the plain cotton, teasing her so thoroughly that she found herself clutching the table so hard she would surely leave indentations.

Calling on all her strength, she tried to stay still, but her body bucked with pleasure, her muscles spasming in a desperate attempt to draw him in, and all she could do was beg. "Please, more. Reece, I want more."

"Say it," he ordered. "Tell me what you want."

"I want you." It was as plain a truth as she'd ever spoken. She was lost in desire, she was craving sensation. He was her whole world in those moments, and all she knew was the way her skin sizzled as electric sparks zinged throughout her body. She was beyond wet now, and she wanted all of him. His fingers. His mouth. His cock.

Some small part of her mind argued that she should protest, because no matter what happened next everything was going to change, and they'd never be Reece and Brent and Jenna again.

She knew that, but she didn't care. Maybe she'd regret it later, but right then all she wanted was Reece. He'd filled her head and fired her body. She had to have him. She *would* have him.

"Fuck me," she finally begged, arching back and surrendering completely.

She'd deal with the fallout later.

Right now, all she wanted was Reece.

Chapter Thirteen

"SAY IT AGAIN," he demanded, his breath hot against her core.

"Fuck me," she demanded, the words no longer terrifying. On the contrary, now they seemed entirely necessary.

"Soon," he promised. "When you're ready."

"Are you insane? Believe me, I'm ready." She was begging, but she didn't care. She craved him, needed him. Felt that she might go mad if she didn't feel him deep inside her.

"No," he said simply as he used his fingertip to pull her panties aside. "You're not," he added, sliding two fingers deep inside her.

She gasped, then bit down on her lower lip so hard she drew blood.

His tongue flicked over her clit, sucking and teasing as the fingers of one hand thrust inside her. With his other hand, he reached up and found her breast, still half-in and half-out of her bra. And as he teased her clit with his tongue, he squeezed her nipple with his fingers, the ministrations sending a current of sexual heat from her breast to her clit, so sharp and vibrant that she almost couldn't stand it.

She squirmed, trying to calm the raging sensations. Or maybe not to calm them. Maybe she was trying to take them higher. Further. She didn't know. All she knew was pleasure. All she knew was need.

And as he sucked harder, teasing her mercilessly, she ground against his mouth, her hips gyrating as he teased and sucked. His beard scraped her sensitive skin, adding to the glorious sensations and making electricity rise to the surface of her skin, pooling and buzzing, and gathering in strength until everything seemed to coalesce in one perfect, sweet circle.

One tiny nub of pure magic that hovered, glowing on the edges of her consciousness before finally, brutally, bursting apart in a firestorm of sensation so intense it turned her inside out and thrust her all the way to the stars.

She seemed to take forever for the bits of her to merge back together, but when she finally returned to herself, she found him looking at her with a very self-satisfied grin.

"Now," he said. "Now, I know you're ready."

REECE FELT the power of Jenna's orgasm break through him. The explosion of passion. The wildness of complete release. The near-pain sounds of pleasure as she cried out. All of it combined to make him so fucking hard he knew that if the didn't take her right then, he'd probably implode on the spot.

"Jenna." Her name tasted like honey. "Baby, I have to—"

"God, yes." Her voice was strained. "Please, Reece. Please. I want you inside me."

He wouldn't have thought it was possible, but he got even harder in response to her obvious need. "Slide down," he ordered, grabbing her hips before she had time to comply and pulling her to him. She was deliciously wet, and as he held her hips in place on the desk, she put her arms around his neck.

"Hard," she whispered. "Please, Reece. Don't be gentle."

He couldn't even form words. He could only comply. He'd brought a condom with him, and now he slipped it on. Then he thrust his hips forward, driving himself into her, even as he pulled her toward him, his fingers clutching her perfect ass.

Her head was tucked in near his neck, and gasped and pleaded and moaned as he took her deep and hard and fast. She was tight, so tight that he couldn't tell where he ended and she began. He glanced down, watching his cock disappear inside her slick folds, and moaned with growing pleasure.

So close. He could feel the explosion coming. His balls tightening, his body readying for release. He wanted her to come with him, but he didn't want to stop the rhythm. "Touch yourself," he ordered. "Play with your clit. Come with me."

She complied obediently, her hand slipping between their bodies, and he watched, mesmerized as she teased her clit while he fucked her, her fingertip sliding down to brush his cock with every few thrusts.

"Reece," she murmured. "Oh, Reece, I'm close."

She didn't have to tell him; he could feel the way her pussy was clenching, tighter and tighter as her orgasm approached.

"Come on baby. Come with me. Explode with me, sweetheart. Come with me now."

On cue, she arched back, her body trembling violently, the sudden movement pushing him over the edge, too. They shattered together, the pieces of their souls dancing and combining together, ensuring that they could never truly be apart again.

"THIS IS AN A-PLUS, PERFECT CHEST." Jenna sighed, the sound so full of contentment it seemed to fill Reece's soul. They'd ended up recuperating on the floor. Now, she rolled over, then straddled him, her finger tracing the lines of his tattoos, the pressure just enough to keep a current of electricity coursing through him and his cock on red alert. "Just so we're clear, this perfect chest is my property now, right?"

"All yours," he assured her, then cupped the back of her head and pulled her down for a kiss to seal the promise.

"Mine to do with as I will," she continued, sliding down his body, and replacing the finger she'd been using to trace his tats with her tongue.

"Christ, Jenna. It's past eleven. We need to put some clothes on before someone gets to work."

"To tease and to enjoy," she continued, ignoring him. "Mine," she repeated, as she let her naked body slide up his, until his cock was nestled against her ass and her mouth brushed over his. She wiggled her hips, and he groaned as his cock stiffened painfully. "That, too, right?"

"Baby, I'm with you one-hundred percent."

She slid her hand down, then stroked him before shifting her hips once again to position the tip of his cock at her entrance. The condom was long gone in the trash, but he was too far gone to even think about stopping her. Besides, he'd been tested recently, and he knew he was clean. And he knew Jenna well enough to know she wouldn't have unprotected sex unless she was, too. "Dominion," she whispered, taking the tip of him inside her. "Control," she continued, sliding further down, taking him in deeper.

She sat up, her hands at his waist, her teeth grazing her lower lip. "Ownership," she said, and in time with the word, she thrust down hard, arching back and taking him all the way inside her.

He lifted his head, saw the way she was pistoning on his cock, and nearly blew his wad right then. But no, he wanted to come with her this time, and he reached down, his fingers finding her clit. "Don't stop," he ordered, painfully aroused by the vision of her naked body riding him, by the sensation of her wet folds against his fingers and the hard, tight nub of her clit. The way her breasts bounced and the sweet, aroused noises she made, like tiny squeaks of passion.

She was close—he could feel it. Her pussy clenching tight around him, her wild yet rhythmic movements. He was close, too. Ready to explode, so close in fact he wasn't sure he could hold back any longer. "Come with me, baby," he ordered, then slid his slick finger around to her backside and slipped it just barely into her tight little ass, and was rewarded by an instantaneous, surprising orgasm.

"Holy crap," she said when she'd stopped gasping. "That was incredible. I've never done that."

"I'm glad. I own you, you know. All of you."

"Oh, yes, you definitely do," she sighed, her body warm against his. Then she pushed herself up and eyed him with renewed purpose. "But to get back to what I was saying before," she began, and he burst out laughing.

"What?"

"Well, it's not that I don't trust you, but I'm not sure why you're putting me to such an evaluation. Then again, maybe I do have an idea. I just hope that I'm wrong."

She grimaced, then rolled to prop herself up on her elbow. "I was just thinking that you're almost as fine as a piece of art. Hell, maybe finer."

"Uh-huh."

"And fine art should be displayed."

"No."

"Reece..." Her voice trailed off into a plea.

"No," he repeated, then pushed himself up onto his elbows. "And unless we want to get caught with our hands in each other's cookie jars, we need to get dressed. Tyree's been coming in early these days.

"Dammit, Reece, don't make me beg. I want you in the calendar contest."

He kissed the tip of her nose. "No."

"But—"

"I'll strip for you, but not for a camera. And definitely not for the crowd at The Fix."

"But—"

He stood up and tugged on his jeans, then looked down to see her naked and pouting on the office floor. "I almost have to get a picture of that," he said, then pretended to reach for his phone.

"Don't you even think about it." She took the hand he offered and let him help her to her feet. His arm went around her waist, and he was struck by how good it felt to hold her like this. Not to mention how delicious it was to have taken her like that in the office. To know that he could have her whenever and however he wanted. *Jenna*. The woman he'd loved his whole life, and who he'd been craving for months.

"What are you thinking?"

"I'm thinking how much I want to bend you over this desk, spank your ass for going on about me parading across that stage, and then fuck you until you come so hard you scream."

"Oh." She swallowed, her eyes wide.

"You asked."

"Yeah. I did." She licked her lips. "Tell me why."

He studied her for a moment, wondering if he'd crossed a line. But he had no desire to play games with her. He knew what he wanted—and that was Jenna.

"Because you're mine. Fully. Completely. Not Easton's. Not anyone else's. Mine to touch. Mine to fuck. Do you understand?"

"Yes." She licked her lips, her eyes glued to him.

"I've wanted you for one hell of a long time, and now that I have you, I don't want to play games anymore. I'll be your friend until the end of time, and I hope you know that. But this—Jenna, I need to know now if what's between us—if how I want to claim you—is going to be too much for you. Because, baby, I don't want to hold back with you. Not ever."

"I see." Once again, she licked her lips, and he had to reach down and shift his cock inside his jeans. Then she took a step toward him, her naked body moving with such grace he wanted to ignore the fact that the rest of the employees would be arriving soon.

When she was only inches from him, she took his hand, spread her legs, and ran his finger over her slick, hot pussy. "It's not too much," she said, her eyes never leaving his. Then she turned and bent over the desk. "I think you better spank me."

"Oh, holy fuck, Jenna."

She didn't say anything. Just spread her legs wider, offering all of herself to him.

Fuck it. He wouldn't deny wanting it. And if she wanted it, too...

He stood behind her, looking at that perfect ass, and then smacked his palm hard and firm against he fleshy part, then rubbed the sting away. "That was to remind you that you're mine." He spanked her again. Then again, cherishing her breathy cries. He slid his hand between her legs and found her so wet now she was practically dripping.

He thrust two fingers inside, then another, fucking her so hard with his fingers that her breasts rubbed the desk. "Do you like that? Getting fucked at the office?"

"Yes."

He spanked her again. "But only by me."

"Yes."

"You shouldn't have seen Easton last night."

She said nothing, and he smacked her again, then once more. "Tell me," he demanded. "Tell me what I want to hear."

"I'm yours," she whispered.

"Do you like the way your ass feels?"

"Yes. But I mostly like the feel of your hand."

He took a moment to absorb her words, treasuring them. "You're mine," he repeated, rubbing the sting out.

She looked at him over her shoulder, then nodded slowly. "Oh, yes." The words were breathy and full of need. "But don't you know that I always have been?"

He lifted a brow. "Is that so?"

"Definitely."

He bent and kissed her. "We should get dressed."

She nodded, then slid her shirt back over her head. "By the way, I didn't go out with Easton last night."

His brows rose. "You didn't?"

"Nope." She finished pulling on her clothes. "I called and canceled. Then I went home, got in bed, slid my hand between my legs, and thought about you."

"Christ, Jenna."

Her smile was playful as she turned and headed toward the door. "Just thought you should know."

"You could have told me before I spanked you."

She paused before leaving the room. "I could have," she agreed, then winked. "But I didn't."

Chapter Fourteen

IT WAS AMAZING what a little sex could do for one's outlook on life, Jenna thought. Before, she'd felt disorganized and lost, now she exuded confidence and ability. She was on-task, on-point, and on her A-game.

And, frankly, feeling pretty smug that she and Reece had both been dressed and business-like when Tyree had strolled into The Fix just after noon.

Now, it was twelve-fifteen, and she was seated at the long table in the back bar, which was doubling as a temporary conference room. She shared the table with Brent, Tyree, Easton, and Reece. The latter sat across from her, a position that she'd intentionally chosen, as the possibility of his thigh or hand brushing hers during the meeting had far too much potential for distraction.

After only a few minutes though, she'd had to reassess that supposition. Because every time she'd looked up, there he was, looking right back at her. Which would have been fine, except that his eyes made her remember the way he'd looked at her naked. And his hands brought back memories of the sensual warmth that spread through her body in the wake of his touch. And his mouth...

Well, she couldn't look at his mouth, because all that did was make her go soft and wet between her legs, and the last thing she needed during her very first partnership meeting was to squirm like a harlot as she tried to battle back a fantasy-induced orgasm.

Once they'd all been seated, Easton had taken point, walking them all through an overview of what they needed to do to formalize the partnership and to make sure the new business ran as planned—and that they were all working toward the goal of increasing profits and repaying the mortgage.

Easton had pulled her aside before they'd begun, and she'd apologized again for breaking their date.

"The night just went kablooey," she said, then explained about the ridiculous job interview. "I would have been terrible company."

He'd sympathized, but he'd also asked her out again. Which, frankly, Jenna hadn't been expecting.

"Oh. Well. Um." She frowned, then told a little white lie, saying that she'd thought more about it, and she just didn't feel comfortable dating him right then.

It was technically true, even while being a big fat lie of omission. It wasn't her fault that he interpreted "right then," to mean while he was acting as the attorney for the new partnership. Because, of course, the real reason was sitting across the table from her.

But Reece and Jenna had already decided that until Brent knew the truth, they couldn't tell anyone. "He'll be fine," Reece had assured her. "So long as he knows we're both all in, he'll be happy for us."

Jenna hoped he was right. Brent was like a brother to

her, and the thought of messing up that relationship was eating at her.

What? Brent mouthed at one point when Easton was describing the nuts and bolts of the partnership agreement.

She just smiled and shook her head, embarrassed to realize she'd been staring at him, dreading the inevitable moment. *Mind wandering,* she'd mouthed back. *Legalese.*

He'd grinned, and she'd said a silent thank you for having pulled off the deception.

In truth, there really was a lot of legalese. During the two-hour meeting, Easton went over the nitpicky details of the partnership as well as the various model releases and other handy-dandy agreements he'd drafted for the calendar contest. He passed around sheaths of paper to each of them, chock full of legal releases, partnership agreements, banking documents, and on and on and on.

He was relentless. To the point where Jenna was happy to sign whatever Easton thrust in front of her, just to stop the madness.

"It's a celebration, that's for sure," Tyree said, once all the ink was dry. "But we still have to pay off the damn mortgage by the end of the year, or else we're right back where we started, only worse. Because you boys will have lost your investments." His expression was tight, reflecting his ongoing fear that everything would fall apart. That they'd all lose the bar, and the guys would lose the money they'd kicked in to finance the campaigns to increase the bar's revenue, the biggest of which was the calendar contest.

A contest that just happened to be Jenna's primary responsibility.

She felt that weight on her shoulders as she stood up

and leaned against the window, facing them all. "It's going to be great," she said, hoping she exuded confidence. "I know we have a ton of customers who want to help. And when we get the word out that one of the reasons for the calendar contest is to keep The Fix open and operating, we'll have even more support."

"I'm not sure about that," Tyree said. "You seriously want us to announce that we're in dire straits?"

She met his eyes. "Absolutely. Not that it's dire. But just the facts. The balloon note is due at the end of the year. And if the money isn't there, The Fix will go away. Austin's a town that loves its local institutions. We just need to give the people a reason to support us."

He leaned back, clearly not thrilled with the idea, but he looked from Reece to Brent in turn, and when they both nodded, he shifted his attention to Easton. "Well, counselor? You see a downside to this?"

"Honestly, no. There's a whole population of Austinites who'll want to help a place like The Fix stay open. Good food, awesome drinks, great service, and a music line-up that includes lots of local bands. Get the word out, and they'll come. And if they don't..." He trailed off with a shrug. "Well, that's something you need to know, too, right?"

Tyree didn't answer immediately, but he nodded slowly. Finally, he looked up at Jenna. "Fine. But we're sharing facts, not weaving sob stories."

"Exactly," she confirmed. "And keep in mind, the calendar contest is only one arm of the octopus. We've got new marketing ideas, other ways to monetize. A whole laundry list of marketing goodness. In fact, we're starting full-blown on Saturday at Eeyore's Birthday Party," she added, referencing the annual Austin event where The Fix was going to have a stall selling beer, drinks, and limited snacks. "I'll have flyers letting folks know that an expanded menu is in the works, and also advertising the contest. So expect sign-ups by next week."

She moved behind Tyree and put one hand on his shoulder. "In other words, we've got this." Her eyes met Reece's as she spoke. "You just have to have faith."

"And with the four of us leading the charge," Reece added, "there's no way we'll fail."

"Ted Henry might have something to say about that," Tyree said, referring to the man who'd made him the original loan. A man who Easton had learned just happened to be one of the major investors in Bodacious and its related bars and restaurants.

"Ted Henry's a two-faced bastard who'll end up getting exactly what's coming to him," Brent said. "I keep telling Faith that bad guys get their comeuppance. I'm not letting the prick make a liar out of me."

"I say we drink to that," Tyree said. "Reece, you want to do the honors?"

"Hell yes," he said, then went behind the bar and came back with a tray topped with five pints. They raised their glasses, and Tyree looked at each of them in turn. "To the best friends a guy could hope to have."

"Right back at you," Brent said. He glanced at his watch. "And since we open in about an hour, I think it's time we all get to work. So we can keep our promises to earn shit tons of money over the next seven months."

"Deal," Jenna said, just before Aly poked her head in and waved for attention.

"Sorry to interrupt, but there's a woman here who says she's supposed to meet with Jen. Her name's Maia?"

"Be right there," Jen said. Then to Tyree, she added, "See? I told you your regulars want to help."

"That girl's a sweetheart," Tyree said. "Been coming here since she was an undergrad."

"We met in grad school," Jenna told him a few minutes later, when the two of them walked out to meet the vibrant black woman who hurried over to greet them, the beads on the ends of her tiny braids flashing in the bar's dim morning lighting.

"I'd love to officially work with Jen on all of this," Maia told Tyree after she'd given him a hug in greeting. "But we're doing an event for the corporation that owns Bodacious." She grimaced. "Conflict. But I've got all sorts of contacts to share with Jen. And," she added, "I have some ideas about bringing in talent. And there's no conflict issue when I'm just shooting the shit with a friend."

"Don't you do anything to get in trouble," he said.

Maia pressed her hand against her chest and fluttered her eyes. "Me? Perish the thought. Now go away," she added, waving him off. "Go be productive and let us talk."

He chuckled but did as she ordered. "You're sure it's okay?" Jenna asked again, once he was out of earshot.

"Sweetie, I never do anything that would mess with my business. Especially not so soon after making partner. But helping a friend? Helping to keep my favorite bar's doors open? I mean, this is the place that helped me make partner in the first place. If my former boss weren't so busy with her touring schedule, then she'd still be a solo act, and I'd be an employee. But Tyree let her perform, and her career took off. And now here I am in all my marketing glory."

"Fair enough," Jenna said, laughing. And Maia did have a point. Her partner was Cam's sister, Kiki King, a singer/songwriter in Pink Chameleon, a Grammy award-winning band.

"Speaking of, PC's on tour right now, but I *think* they

might be able to perform in October for the wrap-up of your calendar contest."

"That would be amazing," Jenna said. She and the guys had agreed that the twelve events would be held on alternating Wednesdays, with the competition for Mr. January taking place on the third Wednesday in May. Just two and a half short weeks away.

"Actually, I wanted to talk to you about the schedule," she told Maia. "I figure we need to build excitement with each of the twelve contests. I don't want interest to lag, so we have to get more and more creative over the course of the twelve events."

"That would be my advice," Maia said, pushing her purple glasses higher on her nose. "You want to start with a bang, of course, but at the same time, you want excitement to build. Because falling enthusiasm will be a death blow to success."

"But no pressure," Jenna said, and they both laughed. Aly came over then to take their lunch orders, and the conversation shifted to nitty-gritty things like how exactly to build that magical excitement, which printers in town were reliable, which morning TV shows were always looking for content, and which local celebrities might be induced to enter the contest. Or, if not that, to promote either the contest or The Fix itself.

By the time Maia said she had to run, Jenna felt ridiculously optimistic. Like maybe she had a handle on all of this. Like maybe everything was going to turn out okay.

She stayed at the table for another couple of hours, her laptop in front of her as she shot off email after email and filled her electronic to-do list with so many tasks it was a wonder her computer didn't howl in protest.

"You're looking very productive."

She twisted in her chair, smiling, as Reece laid his

hand on her shoulder. "That's because I'm kicking ass and taking names. I've pretty much got feelers out to the whole city at this point. Before I'm done, we'll have local celebrities as contestants, local female celebrities as judges, and every person in the city stumbling all over themselves to get coveted tickets to the Wednesday night contests."

"Tickets?"

"We have to have a way to control the door. I figure we give some away—I'm thinking radio as one possibility—but charge a premium for the rest. There's more panache with a price tag."

He bent over and kissed her head. "I love the way you think."

"Reece!"

She scooted her chair away from him as she shot to her feet, her eyes scanning the bar for Brent. For anyone who might have noticed the kiss.

"He's in the office talking with Tyree," Reece said, reading her mind.

"But Aly and Eric and Tiffany are here," Jenna said, heading toward the back of the bar and the door that led to the alley. "We have to be careful," she added. But as soon as the service door shut behind them, she was in his arms, sighing against his chest as he held her tight, one hand lightly cupping her ass as the other rubbed gentle circles on her back.

"Come home with me tonight," he said.

"Soon," she promised, as nerves twisted her stomach.

He cupped her chin. "He loves us both, Jen. If he's upset, it'll be with me. But at the end of the day, he'll be okay with it."

"Maybe." She wanted to believe him, but she couldn't shake the fear. Reece and Brent were her family. The only family she had near here now that her mom had moved away.

And even though she trusted Brent with all her heart and loved him like a brother, Jenna knew only too well that even family can let you down. And the people who claim to love you can leave just like everyone else.

Chapter Fifteen

EEYORE'S BIRTHDAY PARTY had been held in Central Austin's Pease Park on the last Saturday of April for longer than Jenna had been alive. And she'd been a regular attendee all her life, having missed only two that she could recall. Last year, when she'd been in LA interviewing for jobs, and her sophomore year of high school, when she'd been in the hospital recovering from an emergency appendectomy.

Founded in honor of the gloomy character from the Winnie the Pooh books by A.A. Milne, the party had grown from a simple gathering that some University students had put together to an event so large it sometimes seemed that the whole town turned out. Including, always, a flower-draped donkey as the donkey-of-honor.

All proceeds from the event went to various non-profit organizations, and dozens upon dozens of local vendors showed up with games, crafts, food, and enough drinks to keep the party going. Even in the new millennium, the party had a hippie vibe, and it was much more kid-friendly in the early hours when children and adults lined up for face-painting, giant soap bubble games, kites, henna tattoos, and lots and lots of costumes.

"There he is!" Faith called, jerking free of Jenna's hand so she could run pell-mell across the park toward where this year's Eeyore stood inside a pen looking appropriately gloomy.

Jenna squeezed Reece's hand. "What time are we supposed to relieve Brent?"

He glanced at his watch. "Soon. But he knows what we've got on our hands," he added, with a nod toward Faith, who had entered the pen and was gently stroking the donkey's nose. "He won't care if we're a little late."

Brent was currently manning the booth that The Fix on Sixth was sponsoring, selling beer, wine, and a limited selection from the menu, with this year's proceeds benefitting the Austin Zoo, a small local zoo dedicated to animal rescue and rehabilitation. Jenna had loaded him and the rest of the staff up with stacks of flyers announcing The Fix on Sixth's Man of the Month calendar model contest, and giving details on both how to sign up and when the contest would be running live on stage.

"Maybe we should be a lot late," Jenna said as she and Reece parked themselves by the pen's exit. Then she turned in his arms and tilted her face up for a kiss. She and Faith had gotten their faces painted less than an hour before, and glittery pink rubbed off on Reece's nose. She wiped it away with her thumb. "We could enlist Elijah to watch Faith, and you and I could go escape into the trees." Not that there were many trees where they were, but Jenna was motivated enough to walk a ways if it meant some privacy with Reece.

"Tempting," he said. "How about I kiss you again now, and we'll call it a rain check for later?"

"That's a plan I can live with." She rose up on her toes,

her arms going around his neck as she lost herself in the kind of slow, deep, demanding kiss that had her imagining long nights in bed with that tongue doing even more amazing things to her body.

"Well," she said when they broke apart. "Is it later yet?"

His mouth curved up. "Anticipation, baby. It's the best aphrodisiac there is."

"Jenna! Reece! Did you see? I petted Eeyore!" Faith burst out of the gate and ran toward them.

"I know," Jenna said. "Was his nose soft?"

"Uh-huh." She looked between the two of them, her face screwed up with concentration. "Can I be a flower girl?"

"A what?" Reece asked.

"A flower girl."

"Like this?" Jenna pointed to her own face and a colorful flower that curled up near her eye.

"Noooooooo." Faith rolled her eyes. "A real flower girl. Like Missy got to be when her big sister got married last month. I want to be a flower girl, too. Can I be yours? Pretty please?"

"Oh," Jenna said. She glanced at Reece, and her stomach twisted when she saw the tightness on his face. She knew why, of course, and not for the first time, she had to wonder if he'd ever come around on the side of marriage—and what she'd do if he didn't. But she shoved the thought firmly from her head. They'd been a couple for all of twenty-seven seconds, and their best friend didn't even know the truth yet. Marriage was the last thing she needed to be thinking about.

"Please..." Faith's voice rose in a heartfelt plea.

"I have an idea," Jenna began, managing a sideways smile at Reece. "The minute we need a flower girl, you're going to be the one we call. Okay?" The girl's smile widened. And before she could ask when exactly that might be, Jenna grabbed her hand and said, "Why don't we go get henna flower tattoos on our hands right now?"

"Can we?" Faith's eyes went wide.

"Sure. Wouldn't Daddy think that's pretty?"

The little girl nodded, then looked up at Reece. "Are you coming, too, Uncle Reece?"

"I think this sounds like girl-time, okay?"

Faith nodded, her black curls bobbing. "I like girl time," she said. "Someday, I'll have a mommy, and can have it whenever I want."

A knot of tears rose in Jenna's throat, and she blinked furiously to keep them from seeping out through her eyes. "Did your daddy tell you that?"

"Oh, no. Mrs. Westerfield," Faith said, referring to her regular babysitter. "She says Daddy doesn't know what's good for him, but that someday he'll find a nice lady."

Jenna met Reece's eyes, and saw that he looked as help-less as she felt. But then he sank to one knee and pulled Faith close. "Well, I'll tell you what. Until he does, you and Aunt Jenna can have all the girl time you want, okay?"

"Okay," she said agreeably, then stuck one thumb into her mouth and held out her unoccupied hand for Jenna.

"What are you going to do?" Jenna asked, as Reece pulled her close and rested his forehead against hers.

"I'm going to go relieve Brent," he said. "It's not the same, but I think a little daddy-daughter time wouldn't come amiss."

"No," she agreed. "Definitely not."

"Aunt Jenna! Come on!" A little hand tugged hard on her fingers.

"Someone's anxious," she said, letting herself be led away. "We'll find you later," she called back to Reece.

Later turned out to be a full hour since the line for

henna was long and, right next to the henna tent was a small pen filled with peacocks.

"All right, rug rat," Jenna said. "Time to go find Reece."

"Good luck," a familiar voice said, and she looked over her shoulder to see Brent leaning on a nearby post.

"Oh, you're here. Good. Reece is covering The Fix's booth?"

"Tiffany's on it," Brent said. "That's why I came to find you. That, and to check on my junior ornithologist," he added, pointing to Faith, who was creeping up on a preening male peacock.

"We're having a great time," Jenna said. "But what about Reece?"

"He had to go. His dad called. Edie slipped, and she's in the ER."

"Oh no."

"He said he tried to call, but your phone's going straight to voicemail. He thinks you may be out of charge."

She pulled it out of her small shoulder bag and saw that he was right.

"Do you want to go meet him? I know you told Faith that you were going to spend the evening playing with her, but I can smooth that over."

"No. Thanks, but it's okay. I'll check in with him tonight, and I'll go over there and see her tomorrow." She hesitated, then cocked her head to one side. Something was off, but she wasn't sure what.

"I'm not blind," he said, his voice suggesting that he was giving her a clue.

"What are you talking about?"

"You know what I'm talking about," he said. "Why didn't you tell me?"

She hugged herself. "Because I'm an idiot?"

"You?"

"Reece thought we should tell you right away. But I..."

"What?"

"Don't tease me, Brent. You know me too well. I was scared, okay? I love you, too. And this—with Reece, I mean—it changes everything."

"You're right," he said, and her eyes shot to his in shock. "It does change everything."

Her heart was suddenly pounding very hard. "What are you—"

"And you're right that you're an idiot," he continued.

She frowned, confused, but a tiny bit of the terror was lifting. "Am I?"

"Do you think we haven't already survived change? The three of us, I mean?" Before she could answer, he turned and pointed to Faith. "Faith was one hell of a change. Did I lose either of you?"

"No." Her word was barely a whisper. "It's just that I—"

He pulled her roughly to him, his hands on her shoulders, and he stared into her eyes with the same intensity with which she'd seen him look into Faith's. *It's just a nightmare, sweetie. None of it is real.*

"I know," he said to Jenna now. "I know it scares you. I even know why. But you won't lose me."

"You." She turned the word over in her head, examining the implications. "But you think I might lose him?"

He didn't deny it. "Just be careful before you get in too deep."

Her heart skipped a beat, but she understood what he was talking about. How could she not? She knew Reece as well as Brent did—better when you factored in the last couple of days. And she'd seen the way his expression had closed off when Faith mentioned being a flower girl at their wedding.

"I went in with eyes open," she told Brent. "And we've just barely gone from friends to lovers."

"All I'm saying is to be careful. And to be sure what you want—and what you're willing to settle for—before you get too deep."

She managed a sideways smile. "No worries. I'm already treading water. And the truth is, I'm a damn good swimmer."

Chapter Sixteen

IT WAS six in the morning when Jenna let herself into Reece's apartment. She'd considered going during the night, but she wasn't sure if he'd still be at the hospital with Edie and his dad. And besides, she'd wanted a few hours to get a handle on her thoughts.

Now that she'd managed that, she was done waiting.

She hadn't bothered knocking, nor did she bother calling out once she was inside. The garage apartment was tiny, with a loft-style bedroom over part of the living area, a kitchen tucked into a sunlit corner, and a decent sized bathroom on the opposite side of the space.

That's where Reece was. He'd left the door slightly open, and steam from his shower escaped into the apartment, a swirl of white mist that seemed to draw her near. She could smell him. Or his soap, at least. A clean, masculine scent. And when she pushed the door open and stood on the threshold, she could see his outline behind the foggy shower door.

For a moment she simply watched him, succumbing to the rush of pure, visceral need that coursed through her, settling between her thighs and making her wet. Then she walked to the stall and opened the door.

"I was wondering if you were going to join me," he said, his back still to her. He turned. "I was hoping you would," he added, and if the state of his erection was any sign, he meant it.

"You knew I was here?" A stupid comment, since obviously, he'd known. She glanced down, saw again how hard he was, and swallowed.

A grin tugged at the corner of his mouth, but his eyes never lost their heat. "Come on in. The water's fine."

"We need to talk."

She thought she saw worry flicker in his eyes, but then he turned off the water. There was a white towel hanging on a rack beside her, and he reached for it, his arm coming within a few inches of her. She didn't move, and she could feel the heat rising off of him.

He dried off, then wrapped the towel around his waist before he stepped past her. He continued into the living room, then sat on the edge of the sofa. The house was built on the crest of a hill, and the garage apartment was the highest point of the property. The living room boasted an east-facing picture window, and the couch sat in the middle of the room, so as to face the rising sun. She stood with her back to the window, so that Reece was the most beautiful thing in her view.

"Tell me." His voice was unusually tight, and she realized with surprise that he was afraid she'd come to tell him that the whole thing was a mistake. She felt a twinge of guilt because that wasn't her purpose at all. But she didn't dispel his misunderstanding right away. Instead, she cherished it, the knowledge that he feared losing her as much as she feared losing him providing a concrete underpinning for the words that were to come.

"Brent knows," she said. The announcement was only a preamble, but from his expression, she could tell that he thought that was her primary purpose.

"I know," he said. "He called me last night."

"He did?"

"Told me it was between you and me, that he thought we were good together, and that if I hurt you, he'd rip my balls off and feed them to Gregor," he concluded, referring to Mrs. W's German Shepard.

"Oh." She grinned, a fresh sense of relief washing over her with the knowledge that Brent had given his blessing to both of them. "That's great. But it wasn't what I came over to tell you."

"No? Why did you come?"

"To tell you that you're an ass."

For a second, he just stared at her. Then he nodded, the corner of his mouth twitching as he fought not to laugh. "You're not the first one to say so."

"I mean it. I saw the look on your face yesterday. All that talk of flower girls. You looked like you wanted to sprint across the park and find a bolt hole."

"Did I?"

She lifted a shoulder. "Maybe not quite that obvious, but I knew that you were watching me. Like I was a time bomb just waiting to spew rice and floral arrangements and embossed invitations."

He leaned back, his legs spread just a bit, offering her a teasing view of the shadow beneath the towel and between his thighs. She cleared her throat and forced herself to look at his eyes. And nowhere else.

"I don't have illusions," she said. "Hopes, maybe, but I know that marriage isn't on your radar. I know the man you are, Reece, and I know the way you look at the world. Probably better than anyone else. Most of all, I know that you love me. Hell, I even know that you like me."

"Jenna..." He leaned forward, clearly about to stand up and come to her, but she held her hand out to stop him.

"No. Let me finish. The thing is, I'm not looking for the world right now. I'm not an idiot. I know we're just starting this journey. All I want is to look into the future and see you standing beside me."

"Baby, I've never been anywhere else."

"I believe you. I guess I just want to know that's not going to change."

"Come here," he said, beckoning to her. She walked to him, and he turned her around, then put his hands on her hips as she faced the window. "Do you see that? The morning light breaking through the trees? The vibrant colors? The promise of a new day?"

She nodded, wordless.

"That's how I feel about you. That connection between the light and the world, it's magical. And it's us, baby." He was still seated, and now he turned her around, then lifted her T-shirt and kissed her belly. "I love you. And I need you. And you can hold that in your heart right now as my vow to you for our future."

I love you. He hadn't said the words before, and the way he spoke them now—without any fanfare, as if he'd said them dozens of times to her—made her heart swell, because that reinforced how deep the feeling went. How much their shared past played into a shared future.

"I love you, too," she said. "And for right now, this is all I need, too."

She saw a shadow flicker in his eye and wished she could take back the words. She'd thought that was what he'd meant when he talked about holding what they had in her heart, and that he was making a vow for their future.

That it was his way of telling her that he hadn't dismissed the idea of marriage out of hand, even though it was scary and foreign to him.

But seeing that flicker, she feared she was wrong. More important, she was afraid that after taking three steps forward together, she'd just yanked them both two steps back.

She wished desperately that he felt differently, but she truly understood how ingrained his marriage phobia was. And, understanding, she could adjust. For now, anyway. Because surely as the relationship grew, his fear would dissipate and he'd want more.

Wouldn't he?

She stepped closer, then slipped out of her canvas flats. She kicked them away, then unbuttoned her jeans, watching his face as she wriggled out of them, pulling her panties off at the same time.

"Jenna," he began, but she pressed a finger to his lips, then bent down to unfasten the towel from around his hip. She spread it open on the couch, exposing all of him, including his cock that was already with the program, despite the question in Reece's voice.

Slowly, she straddled him, her hands on his shoulders as she moved her hips so that the tip of his erection teased her entrance. He understood the game and didn't say a word, but his low groan when she lowered herself and took him in held a world of meaning and the promise of a life-time of shared passion. "Make me feel it," she whispered as they moved together. "That connection. The light and the earth."

He didn't disappoint. They started slow, but his hands soon moved to her hips, and their rhythm increased, wild and frantic, like charged particles colliding with each other. Hotter and faster until the conclusion was inevitable and her body burst apart in an explosion of stars.

"I love you," he said again as she clung to him tight. His voice was low, but the deep timbre of his voice rumbled through her, and she sighed, contented. She was happy. Safe. Loved.

And there was no reason to believe that Reece would ever let her down.

"SO YOU TWO ARE DATING NOW," Edie said, positively beaming, her foot in a boot to aid recovery of what turned out to be a nasty sprain.

Jenna glanced at Reece, wondering if he was going to be casually vague about the change in their relationship. But his smile was broad, and he slipped his arm around her waist. "Hell, yes, we are. Did Brent tell you?" His stance shifted so he could face his father, who held up his hands in silent surrender.

"Don't be silly," Edie said. "It's all over the both of you, and I think it's about time."

"I'm in perfect agreement," Reece said, as he pulled out a chair for Jenna. Edie was already seated at the breakfast table, and she reached over to squeeze Jenna's hand. "Welcome to the family, sweetie," she said, and Jenna's heart twisted a little more. Edie and Charlie weren't married either, and after three marriages already, she sincerely doubted Charlie would propose. Or, if he did, that Edie would accept.

"Can I get you a coffee, Edie?" Reece asked, as he put a cup in front of Jenna, who smiled up in surprised gratitude.

"I've got it," Charlie said. "One sugar, one large dollop

of heavy cream." He delivered the same to her, then kissed her on the cheek. "And I'll have your omelet ready just as soon as the toast pops up—oh, there we go." He spun around, back to the counter where two pieces of whole wheat toast had appeared in the gleaming stainless steel toaster.

Edie shot him a warm look. "He's been doting on me all morning. All last night, too."

"You deserve it," Charlie said. He looked at Jenna, and she saw the pain in his eyes. "I thought I'd lost her."

"Fiddle-faddle," Edie announced. "I fell and ended up in the waiting room just to find out I have a sprained ankle. I'm not going anywhere. Not until I see how those turn out," she added, pointing to the kitchen cabinets that Reece was refinishing.

He laughed. "In that case, I'll go as slow as I can."

"Of course, I could say the same thing," Edie said, and everyone looked at her, confused. "About almost losing someone," she said by way of clarification. She pointed at Charlie. "Every day when you go outside and smoke one of those horrible cigarettes, you take a step further away from me. And don't even try to argue that you don't."

"Good luck with that, Edie," Reece said. "I've been trying to get him to quit since I was a kid. So has pretty much everyone he's ever known across the state of Texas. No go."

"A man needs his vices," Charlie said. "Now drop it, you two."

Edie met Reece's eyes, but she just shook her head and said nothing else.

"What are you two kids doing this morning?" Charlie asked, sliding breakfast in front of Edie and obviously hoping to finalize the change in subject.

"I'm not scheduled at The Fix today," Reece said. "So I

thought I might take Jenna to the Botanical Gardens. A long walk and then a coffee." He took her hand and squeezed. "A little romance in the morning. Who knows where it might lead in the afternoon?"

"That sounds amazing," she said. "And unfortunately impossible. I told Brent I'd babysit all day," she added, in response to his questioning look. "I figured I could carve out some time on my laptop and work on all my projects for The Fix. And get my resume out there into the wild," she added, her mouth scrunching up with annoyance. She hated looking for a job, especially when the nibbles were few and far between.

"I talked with Brent and Tyree about that at the park," Reece said. "We can't pay a lot, but it's ridiculous for you to be volunteering your time when the three of us are on payroll. We're all partners, after all."

"Reece, no. We need the funds to finance—"

"You need to eat. And we need a viable business, not one that's so tight that key jobs have to be handled by volunteers. Take the job, Jenna. Otherwise, we're going to hire someone else."

She lifted a brow. "Like you said, I'm a partner, too. Don't I get to decide about hiring someone else?"

"You are. And no. We're three-to-one, which means the men win. Like I said, crappy pay. But a job. And it's yours."

She considered protesting a bit more for form, but the truth was that he was right. The job she was doing filled a position that needed to exist at The Fix anyway. And, from a more pragmatic point of view, she'd pretty much run out of money. It was either accept the job or dive into the lucrative world of bank robbery. Probably not a great option.

"You're all idiots," she said. "But I accept."

"Excellent. And my ulterior motive is that now you

don't have to spend hours sending out resumes. We can do something today."

"I told you. I'm watching Faith."

"Something like the Austin Zoo."

"Yeah?" She hadn't been to the local zoo in years, and the last time she went with Faith, the little girl had been in a stroller.

"We see the animals, we ride the train, then we come home, curl up on the couch, and watch *The Aristocats.* And when Faith falls asleep, we turn off the television. Or we watch something with a different kind of romance..."

"Ooooh," Edie said. "Sugar, you need to take the boy up on that."

"Absolutely," Jenna said. "I'm no fool."

THE ZOO WAS EVEN MORE fun with a little girl who could travel under her own power, though Jenna had to admit she was exhausted keeping up with the kid, who ran from pen to pen trying to decide which of the zoo's rescued animals was the cutest.

The ultimate verdict was a genet, an animal that Jenna had never heard of before, but had to admit was adorable with its catlike features. Since there was no stuffed genet in the store, however, Faith ended up going home with a stuffed lemur she named Cracker Jack, for reasons that weren't clear to either Jenna or Reece.

"I'm exhausted," Jenna confessed as they snuggled on the couch, now comfortable in T-shirts and sweatpants, the little girl between them.

"Welcome to parenthood," Reece said, and she laughed. But she couldn't help wondering if they'd ever be parents. And what would their child's name be if they didn't ever get married?

The unwelcome thoughts pushed Jenna to her feet. "I'm going to make some coffee. Want one?"

He gave her a thumbs-up, then relented to Faith's orders to sing along.

With the two of them belting out *Everybody Wants To Be A Cat*, she disappeared into the kitchen and started measuring grounds into the filter basket.

She'd just pushed the button to start the coffee maker when her phone rang, and she pulled it out of her back pocket, then hurried to answer when she saw the Caller ID.

"Mom!"

"Hi, sweetie."

"Are you in town?" Her mom had mentioned possibly coming back to Texas with Doug, her husband, in the spring for a romantic weekend in the Hill Country.

"Not until summer," she said. "Doug's work schedule is a mess. But I'll give you plenty of notice. We're both looking forward to seeing you. I miss my baby girl."

"Is that why you called?"

"Isn't that reason enough?"

"Of course," Jenna said, laughing.

"Well, I do miss you. But I want to hear how the trip home from California went. And what's this about The Fix?"

Jenna had left a brief message on her mom's voicemail right after the guys had proposed the partnership arrangement. Now, she explained in more detail.

"I think that's wonderful," her mom said. "I don't know what I could do from Florida, but if you need help, all you have to do is holler."

"I know," Jenna said. Her mom had always been

157

mother and father to her. And, in many ways, her best girl-friend, too. "How's Doug?"

"So wonderful." Her mom didn't need to say anymore. The depth of feeling was evident in her tone.

"Was it worth the wait?" Jenna asked. "To get married, I mean."

"Well, I didn't know Doug before, so it's a moot question. And your dad was a nice guy, but he wasn't *my* guy, so it would have been a mistake to marry him." *Even if that was a possibility,* her tone seemed to suggest. "But if I'd met Doug back then, but not married him until now...well, that would be sad, wouldn't it?"

"Yeah," Jenna agreed as an invisible fist grabbed her heart. "It would."

"Why the deep questions?"

"Oh, nothing. Seen any good movies lately?" Her mom loved film and saw most movies on opening day. So it seemed like a good way to change the conversation.

She was right, and they continued to talk for another half hour before Jenna remembered the coffee and they said their goodbyes.

She poured a cup for Reece and herself, then headed back toward the living room, only to find the man and the little girl stretched out on the sofa, both fast asleep.

Jenna carried Faith to her bed, but doing the same for Reece wasn't possible. So she covered him with a blanket, turned out the light, and slipped away to Brent's bedroom, where he'd insisted she sleep tonight since he was getting home so late anyway.

She considered digging in her bag for her laptop, then told herself she'd do it in a minute, after she closed her eyes and relaxed for just a little bit.

The next thing she knew, she felt a heavy weight on her, a hand on her breast, and warm breath on her ear.

She opened her eyes to find Reece on top of her, her shirt pulled up, and his hand working a lovely kind of magic on her body.

"You were asleep," she accused.

"And now I have a second wind. Objections?"

"None at all." She closed her eyes and succumbed to the pleasure of his touch—then yelped when the door burst open and, almost simultaneously, Reece tossed the quilt over the two of them, effectively hiding any lingering nakedness.

Under the quilt, Jenna tugged her shirt down, then sat up. "Hey, kiddo. What's wrong?"

Her thumb escaped her mouth long enough for Faith to announce, "I had a bad dream."

Jenna and Reece exchanged looks, and then he patted the bed beside him. "Come on up here, then."

"Can I sleep here with you tonight?" She snuggled under the covers between them, and grabbed each of their hands. "Please?"

"Of course you can," Reece said, with a tiny smile for Jenna. And when he bent to kiss the little girl's head, Jenna's heart did a little flip-flop, and she knew in that moment what it was like to fall even deeper in love.

REECE WOKE to soft curves and realized that Faith wasn't snuggled up against him anymore. Instead, the warm body beside him belonged to Jenna—*and to him*—and he pulled her closer, cherishing the knowledge that she was truly his now.

He tried to drift back to sleep, but something kept tugging at the back of his mind. Something he needed to do. To check. Something that might be bad if—

Faith!

In an instant, he was bolt upright and reaching for the bedside lamp.

And less than a second later, he saw Brent leaning against the open door.

Relief flooded through Reece, but he scowled anyway. "Don't you knock?"

"I did." Amusement danced in Brent's eyes, illuminated by the soft glow of the lamp. In the bed, Jenna stirred but didn't wake.

"I knocked," Brent continued. "And my little girl answered."

As if on cue, Faith appeared beside Brent. She tugged on his *The Fix on Sixth* tee, then announced, "We watched wrist cats last night!"

"Did you?" Brent scooped his daughter up into his arms. "So I guess you're going to be a permanent fixture around here now?" The question was directed toward Reece, but Brent wasn't quite looking at him. Reece twisted in bed, glancing back over his shoulder to where Jenna was now propped up against her pillow, newly awake and looking delicious with her soft features and sleep-tousled hair.

She smiled at him, and he felt a pleasant kick to his heart.

"Actually," Reece said, turning his attention back to Brent, "I thought I might steal her away. My apartment's small, but cozy. And it could use a woman's touch. Lingerie drying over the shower bar. Face powder in the sink. That kind of thing."

"Jerk," Jenna said and gave his ass a little kick with the ball of her foot.

He laughed. "I stand accused," he said. "But what do you say? Want to move in with me?"

She rolled her eyes as she looked at Brent. "You see what I put up with?"

"I only see a live-in babysitter walking away from me."

"You're going away?" The thumb came out of Faith's mouth long enough for her to ask the question.

"Oh, sweetie. I won't go too far. You know I'd never leave you. Even when I was in LA, didn't we talk on the phone all the time? And now I live in Austin again, so I'll be around to babysit whenever your daddy needs me."

"Promise?" Brent asked.

"Promise?" Faith echoed.

"Sure do," she said, cocking her head toward Reece. "I might even bring a helper."

"Pinkie swear?" Faith begged. And in an echo of their childhood ritual, Jenna, Reece, and Brent knelt on the bed and pinkie-swore with Faith that Jenna and Reece would always be there when her dad needed them. Just like they'd always been before.

Chapter Seventeen

"THAT'S another three hundred calendars sold," Tiffany said, practically skipping up to the corner table where Maia and Jenna were huddled behind Jenna's laptop. "One of the stores on South Congress said they want to carry them. They're getting them wholesale, but—"

"But nothing," Jenna said. "That's great. Thanks, Tiff."

"Are you kidding? You don't have to thank me. This is so awesome. Anything I can do to keep this place open. Not to mention my job," she added before bouncing back to the bar to pick up a tray that was ready. It was ten on a Wednesday night, and the bar was hopping at about ninety percent capacity with a local singer performing on stage, just him and his guitar.

"Pretty soon this place will be at a hundred and twenty percent," Maia said. "You've been kicking butt and taking names getting ready for this thing."

"I can't believe how fast the time has flown by. And how much we've gotten accomplished. Thanks for all your help. Seriously." Jenna raised her wine glass in a toast, which Maia returned enthusiastically.

"My pleasure," Maia said. "I wish I could do more. You feeling pretty confident?"

"I am. I mean, I think the calendar orders are a good sign that the contest will be popular. And we've almost sold out the door for the Mr. January contest. It should be a good event, too. We've had a lot of guys sign up for the contest, and the ones selected to compete are pretty hot."

"You're using local celebrities to pre-select from all the candidates, right?" Maia asked. "I mean, they anoint the ones who'll parade across the stage?"

"Exactly. And then the actual winner is chosen by customer ballots the night of. That way we vet the entrants, but the public feels involved, too."

"And our guys? Tyree and Brent and Reece?"

"They all said no. Bastards." Jenna rolled her eyes. "They claim they have a conflict of interest. I think they're grasping at excuses."

Maia laughed. "Probably. Too bad, though. I'd love to see Tyree parade across the stage without a shirt. That man is completely lickable." She tilted her head to the side, her lips slightly pursed. "I take it back. They're all three totally lickable."

Jenna laughed. "Don't worry. The guys competing are, too."

"And you're doing the rolling thing you told me about? So if a guy doesn't win, he gets to compete for the next month if he wants to?"

"Yup. Which is good, because we have a few local celebrities signed up for January. So if they don't win, they'll still be pushing the contest on their social media accounts come time for the Mr. February contest."

"What other publicity's in the pipe?"

"We've got television coming for Mr. January," Jenna said, completely giddy over that recent coup. "Honestly,

I've been working almost nonstop since we started this project. At least it's paying off. I just hope it pays off enough to keep the bar open next year."

"Positive attitude."

"I know. And I am. I mean, I do. It's just a little frustrating. I mean, I barely see Reece, and I'm living with him now. Well," she added with a devious grin, "I *do* see a lot of him at night. But the days are just a blur and a wave." She shifted on her chair, enjoying the way her muscles ached from last night. They'd been sharing his apartment for almost two weeks now, and the transition had been almost seamless. In fact, the only time it had been awkward at all was when he found her vibrator in her bedside table when he was looking for the television remote.

But the moment had shifted from uncomfortable to deliciously inventive when Reece assured her that she didn't need to be embarrassed...so long as she demonstrated for him exactly how she used it.

"I guess it must be going well," Maia commented, her voice tinged with laughter. "Honey, redheads shouldn't even try to keep a secret. Your cheeks show way too much."

The blush burned deeper, and Jenna focused on the table top as she ran Maia through the rest of the plans that were in place.

"Amanda set me up with a woman who does small business renovations. There's no way it'll get done by the first contest—we're less than a week away—but I'm hoping that if they can work during the night and in the morning, they can get the renovations done by the Mr. February contest."

"That would be great. When are you meeting her?"

Jenna glanced at her watch. "Any minute. She asked to meet me at night because her schedule is crazy. In fact, I bet that's her..." She trailed off, glancing at the door where a tall, curvy blonde had just entered.

"And that's my cue," Maia said, standing up. "Good luck," she added, then disappeared toward the back of the bar as Jenna waved to Brooke and hurried to her side. "I'm Jenna," she said. "Thanks so much for agreeing to talk with me. Amanda says your work is amazing."

"I love what I do," Brooke said with a wide, easy smile that revealed perfect teeth. Beside her, Jenna felt positively drab in her simple business suit, her red hair pulled back from her face with a single clip.

"Well, we're excited about the possibility of you working with us." She indicated the table, and they both sat down, with Brooke occupying the chair that Maia had just abandoned. "I'm not sure how much Amanda told you, but we're basically doing a facelift on The Fix. We're stepping up an already awesome menu, and we're getting the word out to draw in new customers. And then, in about a week, we're launching what is going to be a truly amazing contest for twelve hot men to be calendar models, and we're organizing an entire ladies' night theme around all twelve contests."

"And as part of that, you want to give the building a bit of a facelift, too."

"You got it. Not too much, but enough that folks notice the improvements. Plus, we want to make the stage a little bigger. Possibly shift the angle so we can get more tables in. More capacity means more income."

"Well, I'd love to work with you."

"It's your rates that I'm concerned about," Jenna admitted. "To be brutally honest, we're trying to do all of this on as limited budget as possible. You see, this whole calendar contest is part of a fundraiser. The bar's mortgage comes due at the end of the year, and..."

She trailed off with a shrug, hoping Brooke would get it. Apparently, she did, because she nodded sagely.

"Normally, I'm a little pricey, I'll admit. But I have a proposal for you. If you agree, it could work out great for both of us."

Jenna leaned back. "Amanda mentioned you were looking for a high profile project."

"I was. I am. And to tell you the truth, The Fix is exactly what I'm looking for."

"Okay. I'm intrigued. Shoot."

"The downside is that I can't get started on the work until after your launch, but we should be underway by the second contest, with renovations on the stage completed by the time you're holding the contest for Mr. June, and full renovations on the interior by the time the contest wraps."

"Oh." Jenna tried not to show her disappointment. "We were hoping for a faster schedule than that, honestly. Maybe if you have a crew willing to work during the night at overtime pay, you could finish before the second contest?"

"I'm afraid not. But," she added quickly, "if you agree to that schedule, then all the work—materials and labor—would be free."

Jenna blinked. "Come again?"

"I'm negotiating with one of the cable networks for a property renovation show. Only instead of houses we'd be doing commercial real estate. And if the project goes, this would be the first property."

"Oh. Wow. But how do you the show would use The Fix? I mean, maybe the producers would rather do a different kind of business."

"To be honest, I already made the pitch. And they think it's perfect. The location. The look. Even the fact that you'll be doing the calendar contest in the background. All that makes for good television."

Jenna had worked in marketing long enough to know that was true.

"And since it's kind of a test run, you'd get the benefit."

"And the downside?" Jenna asked, since that sounded too good to be true.

"Well, it'll probably be a little crazy for at least a couple of episodes, until we find our groove. So you'd have to put up with that. But The Fix would be the center of the show, so the upside is the free advertising."

Jenna gaped at her. "And all I have to do is say yes?"

"Pretty much. To be brutally honest, the network big wigs have to formally say yes, too. But the producers and executives are pushing it, and it's close to getting a green light."

"Close," Jenna repeated. "You mean they're waiting for a thumbs-up from us? From The Fix, I mean."

"Yup," Brooke said, but then her perky smile faded a little. "Well, actually, Spencer has to sign, too. The network is insisting that it be a couples show, so he'd be my on-camera cohort. But it's a no-brainer. This is exactly the kind of project he's been looking for."

"Spencer?"

"Spencer Dean," Brooke said, in a voice that suggested the name explained everything. "He used to have a similar show," she added, seeing Jenna's blank look. "But he quit about a year ago."

"Now he wants to come back?"

"Oh, yeah. In a big way," Brooke said, her blue eyes wide and innocent. After a moment, she cleared her throat. "So there you go. That's it." Her teeth grazed her lower lip. "What do you think? I realize it's not what you were expecting, but—"

"But it's better," Jenna said firmly. "So long as we'll know within the week, The Fix is totally in."

"I SHOULD HAVE TALKED with you and Brent and Tyree first." Jenna paced the small living room as Reece watched, amused. "Do you think they're going to mind?" she asked. "Do you mind?"

"Why would I mind?"

"A film crew inside The Fix. A reality show. That's just the height of tacky. Have you seen some of the catfights that happen on those shows? And they get into everyone's business. It's personally invasive."

He chuckled, then drew her close. "I promise not to slide into a catfight with you or anybody else. And as for invasive, I think that's more *Real Housewives* than Austin renovations."

"Maybe." She stopped pacing. "You think?" She sat down on the couch. "I don't know."

He sat on the coffee table across from her, then took her hands. "Is there something else bothering you? Because from where I'm sitting, the possibility of being the featured attraction on a nationwide show about property renovations—especially when those shows are so damn popular—seems like a pretty sweet deal."

"No—yes. I'm tired. Everything just seems so fuzzy today. I think I'm just tired."

He moved beside her, then felt her forehead.

She smiled, just a little. "I'm not sick."

"You don't feel warm," he confirmed, but he couldn't shake the fingers of worry creeping up his spine. Jenna so rarely got sick, but when she did, it was usually something that put her out of commission for weeks. Mono in high school. Pneumonia in college.

"I'm fine," she repeated, and he realized he was still pressing against her forehead. "Just doing too much."

"And you'll make yourself sick if you keep it up."

"Things to do," she said. "And I'll be over the hump soon."

He made a rough noise in the back of his throat, not sure if he was acknowledging the truth of what she said, or dreading that final push. All he knew was that she was fading, and he needed to take care of her. And at the same time, how?

If a guy was being a dick to her in a bar, he could—and had—told the guy to get lost or lose a tooth.

If her car broke down, he could—and had—rescued her.

If she was hungry, he could feed her. If she was sad, he could cheer her up.

But what could he do if she was sick? Nothing except force-feed her vitamins and make her get some sleep. And with Jenna that was always harder than it should be. Unless...

He got up.

"Where are you going?"

"I'll be right back," he said, then returned with a small glass of water and some pills. "Vitamin C, zinc, and a couple of Ibuprofen, just in case I'm wrong about the fever."

"Reece, please. I don't—"

"Can't hurt. Might help. Swallow them."

She looked at his face, and he knew what she saw there. A message that she denied him at her own peril. "Fine," she said, then took the pills as he went back to the kitchen.

Then he went up to the loft-style bedroom before returning to her.

"What was that about?"

He tilted his head up, but was pleased to see that nothing in the bedroom was visible other than the light cast by the ceiling fan's fixture. "Nothing much," he said. "Just putting you to bed. You're tired, you need sleep. Relaxation."

"I need to get my second wind, check my emails, make sure the contestants have signed model releases, make sure we have—"

"And it'll all be there in the morning. Upstairs. Now. Either you walk, or I carry you, but either way, you're getting in bed."

He could see that she was tempted to make him carry her, and he would have been happy to. But then she glanced toward the spiral staircase, seemed to think better of it, and preceded him up the stairs. When she reached the landing, she stopped with a gasp, then turned around to face him.

He'd turned the fan's light off using the remote halfway up, leaving the only illumination from the candles he'd lit when he'd made his quick trip only moments ago. Now, the room was lit by the glow of four candles on a table that also held a bottle of Cabernet and two wine glasses. It also held four black silk ties and a padded blindfold.

"Oh," she said, her tone rising with a question. But at the same time, her voice held so much heat that he knew he'd made the right decision.

"All for you," he said. "You need to relax. And I'm going to make sure you do."

"Reece..."

"Shhh." He nodded to the bed. "Sit."

She did, and he handed her one of the glasses of wine.

"To you," he said. "And also to laying down, closing your eyes, and forgetting everything except the way I'm going to make you feel."

"Reece, I—" His finger on her lips stopped her words.

"Yes, Reece," he said, grinning.

A smile touched her lips, and she tilted her head in acquiescence. "Yes, sir," she said, with a quirk of a brow.

"Finish your wine," he ordered, then laughed when she swallowed the half-full glass in two quick gulps. He took the glass from her, then knelt in front of her, sipping his own wine as he undressed her. Shoes first, then her jeans, brushing her skin softly as he unfastened the button, enjoying the way she squirmed as he tugged her jeans and panties all the way down before tossing them on a straight back chair. He pulled her *The Fix on Sixth* T-shirt off next, and tossed it aside as well. Then he reached behind her, unfastened her bra, and very deliberately, stroked the sides of her breasts as he pulled it off.

In front of him, her eyes were closed, and her teeth grazed her lower lip. She was seated on the edge of the bed, and her thighs were tight together. He wondered if she was wet, and smiled at the knowledge that if she weren't, she would be soon enough. Because this was about Jenna. About her pleasure.

And he was about to make her melt.

JENNA'S HEAD SPUN—AND not just from the effects of the wine. She was drunk on Reece. On the intoxicating sensations that ricocheted through her body as she stretched out spread-eagled on the bed, tied down by the silk cords that attached her wrists and ankles to the head and footboard.

She'd protested when he'd told her what to do, and then a bit more when he'd come at her with the blindfold. But in truth, it was only for form. She wanted the escape he offered. The promise of sensual delights and exquisite sensations. He told her he was going to make her explode, and then he was going to untie her, cover her, and watch her drift off to sleep.

"For you," he murmured, his lips brushing her ear, and she smiled in delight at the idea of being so very thoroughly taken care of.

He kissed her thoroughly. His mouth teasing all over her body. His beard tickling her skin as his lips found her inner thighs, her waist, the swell of her breasts.

He wasn't anywhere near her core, and yet she felt the throbbing need. She tried to squeeze her thighs together to dull the demanding ache, but it was impossible. She was too tightly bound.

"Just let go," he murmured, as his lips brushed her own. "Just let it take you."

Then he was moving down, lower and lower. His hands on her breasts, his fingers rolling her nipples. His mouth moving inexorably toward her core until, finally, she felt his tongue on her clit, and her hips bucked with a silent demand for more.

And Reece, thank goodness, obeyed.

His tongue. His lips. The scruff of his beard. Suddenly, they were all concentrated between her legs. All driving her crazy.

Expertly, he used his hands to cup her rear, angling her toward him, letting his tongue slide into her folds, then tease her clit. Everything he did was driving her crazy, but it was a slow build. A slow burning fire. But the more he continued, the more she wanted the explosion.

She was horny as hell, there was no other way to

describe it. Her entire body seemed to crave him, and she was wetter than she could ever remember. Her breasts ached, and every inch of her skin was an erogenous zone.

She wanted to move. To touch herself. To alleviate some of the achy, burning need. But she could only endure and enjoy, losing herself in a pleasure so intense it bordered on torture.

His mouth closed over her clit, and he sucked and teased as she moaned with increasing passion, her hips bucking as much as the restraints would allow. He was right. She needed this. Needed to be teased and played and taken. Touched and stroked and used.

Again, she fought against the bindings, but to no avail. She couldn't move. She had no choice but to succumb to the building sensation. Rising and rising until he pushed her all the way—and when the climax broke over her, she knew that he'd been right.

He'd very thoroughly relaxed her.

She was exhausted now. Spent. *Reece.* She tried to whisper his name, but sleep was pulling her under, and she wasn't sure if she'd spoken his name out loud.

It didn't matter. He'd just given her the best present ever. He'd sent her to oblivion on orgasmic wings. And when she woke the next morning, his name was still on her lips.

She was untied, and considering how much she had to pee she appreciated that little fact.

She was alone in bed, though, and she didn't appreciate that.

She rolled over to touch his pillow and found it warm. She also found a note. *Full shift at The Fix today. Left you breakfast tacos in the fridge to microwave. Go to a clinic if you still feel bad. Home after closing. Call if you need anything. Love you, R*

She smiled, loving that he'd thought to get her breakfast. But then the idea of food set in, and her smile faded, replaced by a horrible twisting in her gut.

What the—?

But there was no time for the thought. She raced to the bathroom, collapsed onto her knees in front of the toilet, and barfed her guts up.

Was she sick? Except for her stomach, she felt fine. Great even. So maybe she'd eaten something bad? But what?

She considered the question as she washed up, trying to remember everything she'd eaten last night. Then she headed to the kitchen to make coffee, only to be caught short when the smell of the coffee grinds made her want to bolt back to the bathroom.

Oh, no.

Surely not. But her phone was out and she was dialing Amanda before she could talk herself out of it.

"Not all of us rise with the sun," Amanda said without preamble.

"I think I'm pregnant." There was no trace of sleep in her voice. Now, she was wide awake.

"What? Oh! Okay, we've got this. Just don't panic."

"I'm not. I'm okay." That was true enough. Now that her stomach had calmed down, she felt completely centered. Hell, she felt wonderful.

"Did you take a pregnancy test?" Amanda asked.

"No. It would be too early for one of the drugstore kind to work, anyway, I think. But I feel off. And I've been sick all morning."

"Hmm. Well, that's hardly conclusive. And it could be a stomach bug. I mean, you're on the pill, right?"

"True." Reece had used a condom the first time they slept together, but they'd stopped once she told him about the pill. But the truth was that before Reece, she'd sometimes miss a day. And she never worried too much because she wasn't having sex. The worst that would happen was that her hormones got out of whack.

Had she skipped any the month before she started sleeping with Reece?

She couldn't remember.

"What are you going to do?" Amanda asked when Jenna had relayed that little tidbit.

"Be a mommy." She thought of Faith, and the thought made her smile. A child. *Their* child.

Then she thought of the insanity that was Brent's life as a parent, and the smile faded. "It's not convenient timing, but things work out, right?"

"I still say you're jumping the gun."

"Maybe. And you're right. I mean, it's probably the flu," Jenna said, certainty rising as she mentally reviewed her calendar. "We've only been sleeping together a few weeks. I wouldn't have morning sickness yet."

"My mom said she was sick with me from about a week after conception. So who knows?"

"Great. Thanks."

"When's your period due?" Amanda asked.

Jenna did some quick math. "Right about now," she admitted as the evidence in the *Baby* column grew and grew.

"Right. Well." Amanda cleared her throat. "Oh, we're being ridiculous. Go to one of those walk-in clinics and find out for certain one way or the other."

"I will. I'll do that right now." She drew in a breath, dispelling a wave of joy mixed with panic. "This isn't a big deal. My immune system is worn down from too much work and lack of sleep. That's all."

"Of course it is," Amanda said. "You don't have anything to worry about at all."

Chapter Eighteen

IT WAS ALMOST three in the morning when Reece got home, and Jenna had fallen asleep on the sofa. She blinked groggily when she heard his key in the door, then sat up slowly, her body feeling foreign now. A little bit special. A little bit traitorous. And definitely different.

"Hey, beautiful," he whispered as he came inside. "I didn't expect you to be up. How are you feeling? Did you go to a clinic?"

She nodded.

"Good. Did he give you anything?"

"No." She yawned and sat up, trying to get her mind working again.

"No?" He moved to sit by her on the sofa, then felt her forehead like he had that morning. "No temperature. Did he at least tell you why you feel so crappy? Overwork, like you thought?"

"You're worried about me," she said.

"Of course I am."

She wrapped her arms around his neck and held on tight. "I love you," she whispered as cold dread swept through her. A dread she hated, because what she needed to tell him was good. Or it should be. But Jenna couldn't help but fear that the moment she spoke would go down in history as the beginning of the end.

"I love you, too." His voice was wary, and he gently pushed her back, then studied her face. "If you're not sick, do you want to tell me what exactly *is* the matter? Is it the contest? If there's a snag, don't worry. We'll get it worked out."

She shook her head. "No, everything's going great." That was true, and she was grateful. At the moment, she was only equipped to handle one crisis at a time.

"Then what—"

She shoved up to her feet at the same time that she blurted out, "I'm pregnant."

Her eyes were on his face as she spoke, searching for signs of terror with the same minute inspection with which astronomers study the stars. But she saw nothing amiss. No terror. No disappointment.

All she saw was joy. Well, joy laced with a hint of confusion.

"Baby, that's amazing." He pulled her down to him and cradled her on his lap. "Are you sure? It hasn't been that long, and I thought those tests didn't register until—"

"The doctor drew blood. I'm not far along, but there's no doubt."

"Wow," he said, then pressed a hand against her belly. "How long have you known? You should have called me. I would have met you at the doctor's. There are so many questions—do I need to get you something from the store? Pickles?"

She laughed out loud, the tightness that had begun to build in her chest lessening a bit. "No cravings yet. But when I do, I'll tell you." *Assuming you'll really still be here.*

The thought came unbidden, and she could tell that he saw the reflection of it on her face.

"There is something wrong," he said. "Is it the baby? Could they even know this early? Is that why you didn't call me before? Because if there's something wrong, we'll handle it together."

She noticed that he didn't ask if it was his, and his certainty that she'd been with no one else—even back in LA—warmed her. They fit, dammit. The two of them were a perfect match, like a lock and key.

But if that was true, why was it so hard to talk to him right now?

"There's nothing wrong. And I spent the day thinking. I'm sorry I didn't tell you right away, but I needed time to think."

"It's okay. I get it."

"What you said just now, about handling it together. That's kind of what I want to talk to you about."

He nodded, urging her on, but the words wouldn't come.

"Oh, baby." He took her hands. "Tell me."

"I'm scared." The words weren't even quite a whisper.

"Hey, it's okay. There's nothing to be scared of. Women have been having babies forever."

She almost laughed at that. "True, but that's not what I'm scared of." She drew a deep breath for courage. "I don't want to be my mother. A single mom." She closed her eyes, drawing strength from the next few beats of her heart. "That's not who I am."

Reece's brow furrowed, and his eyes grew hard. "Your mom was alone," he said warily. "But I'll be with you. Right by your side. Whatever you need. Whatever the baby needs. It's us, right? And we're a team."

"A team," she repeated. The word seemed flat.

"A couple then. Or, a trio now. Right?"

She heard the note of urgency in his voice and wanted to reach out and soothe him. She couldn't think straight when she was around Reece, but she had to think straight. She had to because now she was thinking for both her and the baby.

And she'd had all day to think about what she was doing. All day alone in this apartment, pacing and walking and searching her conscience.

He might not like it, but she believed in the path she'd chosen. The only question now was whether or not they'd walk that path together.

"Dammit, Jen. Talk to me."

"I know I'm shifting things around on you without any warning. But this little peanut hit me without any warning, either." She stood up, placing her hand on her belly, and sighed. Here was her strength. No matter what—more than herself, more than Reece—she had to think about what was best for the baby. And that's what she was doing now. For hours and hours, that was all she'd thought about.

But thinking was the easy part. Telling Reece—making him understand too—was the challenge. And one she was terrified he couldn't meet.

"I want ... I used to imagine coming home after school. My mom gardening. My dad fixing a car. I never had that —I want my child to have it."

"He will. She will. I'm not going anywhere. We talked about this."

"No, we didn't. Not really. And maybe that's on me. Maybe I made you think I was okay with not getting married when the truth is, I was only okay with not getting married now."

"It's still now, Jen. Nothing's changed but biology."

She smiled at that. "I suppose that's true. But this

particular bit of biology is the most important thing that's ever going to happen to either of us. And that changes things. Speeds them up, anyway."

She sat back down on the sofa, this time a few feet away so she was less tempted to touch him. Touching wouldn't weaken her resolve, but it would make the break that much more painful if he walked away.

"I said I was okay for then," she continued, keeping her hands in her lap though he reached for her. "But it's not okay forever, and I'm sorry if you got that impression. I believe in marriage. I want the commitment. More than that, I need it. And so does the baby."

"I love you, Jen. I'm as committed as I can get. I will always be there for you. For our child."

"You're committed," she repeated. "Just not committed enough to marry me."

"Don't play that game," he said, his voice as tight as a wire.

Tears clogged her throat, but she was determined not to shed them. "You're my best friend, and you always have been. And now you're my lover, and it's great. But I don't need a best friend. And I don't need a lover. I need a father for my baby."

He stood, propelled to his feet by an emotion so powerful it seemed to roll off him. "I am the baby's father."

"I need a husband."

"The hell you do—have you not met my father? Marriage doesn't solve anything. It's not a magic bullet that makes everything work."

"No, but it is a statement, and it's important. At least it is to me. I need the tradition and the ritual and all of it. I need us to be a family." *She needed to know that he wasn't like her father, and that when the going got truly, seriously, horribly tough, she could count on him to step up.* "And, I'm sorry, but if that's not something you need, then—"

"Don't you dare give me an ultimatum, Jen. Don't even think about threatening to take away my child."

This wasn't working. He wasn't getting it, and he sure as hell wasn't agreeing. But he was angry. So angry it seemed to fill the apartment, and she wished she could curl up and hide in the cushions.

"I'd never do that," she said, forcing her voice to be calm. "Not ever. But if you expect me to respect your inability to say those vows, then you have to respect my need for them."

"I'm not your dad, Jenna. I'm not going to say I love my kid only to disappear out of its life forever."

She blinked, and a tear ran down her cheek. He did know her well, and she could never think that of him. But that didn't change what she wanted. *The promise. The commitment.*

"You promised that you'd always be there for me," she told him.

"I am."

"No," she said. "You're not."

"Jenna—"

"No." She shook her head. "If you don't want to be my husband—if that's not the way you can see yourself—then I think I need to go. I'll always love you, Reece. But I can't be with you. Not like that. Not like this. And I'm afraid that if I stay, you'll wear me down." She wiped away tears. "Because I love you so damn much. But I'll hate myself if I give in. And what kind of a lesson would that be for the baby?"

"Please, Jenna. Don't."

But she had to.

Even though it broke her heart, she had to walk away.

FOR ALMOST A WEEK NOW, Reece had been living in a goddamn haze. Jenna had kicked the foundation out from under him, and his world had fallen apart. And, damn him, he still hadn't managed to figure out a way to put it back together again. Much less to get Jenna back.

God, he missed her.

Every night since she'd left, he'd gone to sleep on the couch, unwilling to go up to the bedroom and face the bed they'd shared.

And every morning he'd come out of sleep groggy, a vision of her beside him filling his head. And then he'd open his eyes and reality would give him a brutal smackdown.

He was alone, and he hated it.

But he also hated the position she'd put him in.

Marriage.

There it was hanging between them, and not even that long after they'd talked about it. And he couldn't wrap his head around why she'd want him to commit to an institution he didn't believe in. One so fraught with risk it was practically a curse.

And now they were both alone.

How the hell was that better? How did being apart make any sense when they were in love? When they were going to have a baby?

She'd moved out that very first night, taking only a single bag with her. She'd returned the next day while he was at work, and he'd come home to find all evidence of her gone. The reality had almost shattered him, but what had truly fucked him up was when Brent had arrived a few minutes later, let himself into the apartment, then settled onto Reece's couch with a beer from Reece's fridge.

And then his friend had had the nerve to tell Reece he needed to take a short leave from The Fix. "You need to stay away until after the contest. Too much stress on Jenna. And Ty and Cam can cover you as manager."

"I have an ownership interest in that place," Reece had said. "I'm not staying away."

"Don't stay away because of the bar. Stay away because of her. She needs space."

"Does she? Well, maybe I need her."

Brent had sighed, then looked at Reece with something like pity. "Don't be an ass, buddy. Not any more than you already have been."

Reece had snapped. "You think I should marry her. You? After everything that happened with Olivia, you're going to champion marriage?" The irony was mind-boggling.

"For the two of you? Yeah, I am. I know you. I know Jenna. And I can see clearly even if you can't."

Reece had walked out of his own apartment. The last thing he'd needed was Brent quarterbacking his life from the sideline.

It had taken him a day or two, but he'd cooled down, and he went to Brent's house to see her. She wasn't there.

"She said she didn't want to put herself between us," Brent said as Reece hoisted Faith, then held her strong little body close. "She's staying with Amanda."

"Did you and Aunt Jenna have a fight?" Faith asked.

"Not a fight," Reece told her. "A philosophical difference."

"What's that?" she'd asked.

"The same thing as a fight, as far as I'm concerned," Brent had said. "The end result sure as hell looks the same."

"Daddy! You said hell."

"Yeah, well, sometimes grownups make mistakes." He took the child from Reece's arms. "Sometimes, they can fix them."

After that, Reece had tried to contact Jenna at Amanda's, but she wouldn't answer his calls or texts, and when he called Amanda's business line, Jenna still wouldn't take his call.

"She says to tell you that she's not punishing you," Amanda assured him. "She sent you an email."

Now, the memory clung to him, still raw and painful. He was sitting at his kitchen table, and he pulled out his phone, then pulled up the flagged email for the billionth time.

Reece,

I'm sorry. I know you've tried to reach me, but I just can't. I swear I'm not trying to punish or hurt you by avoiding you. But the truth is that I want you too much to see you.

The thing is, I know how I feel. How I've always felt, and what I've always wanted. I feel what's right, as if the truth were in my bones. But you can make me forget myself, and if I see you, I might cave. You have a certain effect on me...

But this time, I don't want to give in to your demands, and I can't give you everything you want. I know I said I was yours, and I meant it. I still do. If you want to believe I lied to you, then I'm sorry. But I guess that would mean you lied to me, too.

I know you think it's unfair, and I'm sorry for that, too. It just is what it is. I wish you felt differently, because I love you more than I thought was possible.

Give me time, and we can talk. But know this now - I'm not going to change my mind.

Love forever,

Jenna

He read through the email twice more, then snapped out a curse. Although whether he was cursing himself or Jenna, he didn't know.

But tonight was the calendar contest, and whether she liked it or not, he was going to be there. He had to see her, even if he just watched from the sidelines. He had to see her and decide what the hell he was going to do.

That wasn't for a few more hours, though. Until then? Well, he had a truck, and he had a CD player, and at the end of the day, he was Texas born and bred. He was going to put in a CD—classic country, because the songs had to be about broken hearts and lost dreams—and he was going to drive up to Mount Bonnell, the highest point in the city. He was going to sit there and look at the river and feel like a fool for being in such a romantic spot all by himself.

And, dammit, he was going to think.

Determined, he grabbed his keys and headed for the door, only to find his father standing there. He hadn't yet told his dad and Edie about the pregnancy or the fact that Jenna had moved out or about their philosophical difference about marriage. And he didn't want to have that conversation now.

Trouble was, his dad rarely braved the stairs up to the apartment. If he did, it was probably for a heart-to-heart. And that meant that he'd probably noticed Jenna's absence.

"Dad, I—"

"Keep these for me," his dad said, shoving a pack of cigarettes into Reece's hand. "And if you see me with another pack, you call me out. You hear me, son?"

"I—" He glanced down at the pack, and then up to his father. "Yeah, of course. But why?" He'd been on his dad to quit for as long as he could remember.

Something bright lit his father's eyes, but when he answered, he barely smiled. "It's time," his father said. "Sometimes, you just know when it's time to change."

Chapter Nineteen

TONIGHT WAS the contest for Mr. January. The first event of The Fix on Sixth's Man of the Month calendar contest.

It was, Jenna knew, probably the single most important event of her career.

And all she wanted to do was go home, crawl under the covers, and go to sleep.

For days, she'd been working her tail off and battling morning sickness. And neither one of those was as hard or as unpleasant as getting through a day without Reece.

"Am I being an idiot?" she asked Brent for the hundredth time. He was doing a security pre-check for the event and had just finished talking to the doorman and the new bouncers they'd hired. The event had gotten so much press and the tickets had sold out so fast that they were expecting an over-capacity crowd. They'd let people in when space opened, but if folks got rowdy on the street, Brent needed to have a plan in place.

"You're not being an idiot," he assured her. "But why don't we talk about this tomorrow when we're past the contest. I mean, maybe that's a crazy suggestion, but I thought since we both have a checklist about a mile long..."

"I know. You're right. I'm sorry."

His pragmatic pep talk pushed her back into a work groove, and she blasted through a ton of last minute details. She'd hired a graduate student from the drama department at the University of Texas to stage manage the contest, because Jenna wanted to be in the audience in order to gauge the reaction and decide if they needed any design changes. Now Taylor walked Jenna through all of her prep. Her long brown hair was pulled back into an efficient ponytail, and as far as Jenna could tell, Taylor had no worries at all about tonight going off without a hitch.

"We've got this," Taylor said. "Trust me, it's going to be amazing."

The staging area was in the back bar, which was closed for the event. Each man would walk up a red carpet that was being laid right then, climb the stage, take off his shirt, and then say a few words to the audience. Jenna antici- pated that some of them would strip with a flourish, while others would be a bit more subdued. But she'd seen all of their pictures, and she was confident that none would be a dud.

Jenna considered the event's emcee as the greatest coup. Beverly Martin, who'd recently starred in an indie film that was getting a lot of notice. She'd actually approached Jenna, who'd been afraid that she'd have to emcee the contest herself.

When Jenna had asked Beverly why she wanted the gig —and how she'd heard about it—Beverly had been coy. And since Jenna wasn't an idiot, she didn't push. She just said a silent thank you to whatever guardian angel was watching over her, then moved on to the next task.

"You'll go over everything with Beverly? Have we got a teleprompter?"

"It's all good. Chill." Taylor's voice held laughter. "There," she said, pointing. "Isn't that the woman you're meeting with for lunch?"

Jenna followed the line of Taylor's finger and found Brooke. She waved, then pointed to the back table, where Aly had already put out a variety of appetizers.

"Any news?" Jenna asked.

"We're on!" Brooke beamed. "The papers with the network are all signed, and Spencer's on board. And all I had to do was sell my soul."

"What?"

Brooke waved the words away. "Ignore me. I was just trying to be funny."

Jenna had the feeling that wasn't exactly accurate, but she didn't press. "At any rate, congratulations. This is a big deal for you, right?"

"It is," Brooke admitted. "And congrats to you, too. We're going to make this place look amazing."

"Win-win," Jenna said, then stood. "I know I promised you lunch, but let's go find Tyree and tell him."

"Sounds good. And I can't stay for lunch anyway. I've got a million details to work on before we get started. But I'll be here tonight for the contest. I can't wait."

They found Tyree in his office, looking as harried as Jenna felt. Her phone rang right after the introduction, and when she saw that it was her mom, she signaled to Tyree, who assured her that he'd answer any of Brooke's questions, then see her out.

"Mom? Everything okay?"

"Of course. I just wanted to call and wish you luck on your big day."

"Thanks." She tried to sound enthusiastic, but it came

out a little strangled. It *was* a big day. It just seemed a lot smaller without Reece beside her.

"All right," her mom said. "Tell me."

Jenna opened her mouth to tell her mother that everything was fine. But instead, she heard herself asking, "If Doug had wanted to just live with you, would you have done it?"

"Oh, I think so. We're a good match, and it's not like we're going to be starting a family."

"So if you'd met him when he was younger before either of you had kids, you would have insisted on getting married? What if he didn't want to?"

"Jenna, sweetheart. What's going on?"

They were the magic words that opened the floodgate, and she started to tell her mom everything, beginning with the fact that she and Reece were in love.

"But sweetheart, that's wonderful. You know I adore Reece. I always thought you two would make a great couple."

"He doesn't want to get married."

"With his father as a role-model, I'm not sure I blame him."

"But I—" She cut herself off before mentioning the baby. That deserved a longer, more intimate call. Possibly even a weekend trip to Florida for an in-person announcement and celebration. "But it's important to me. And he just completely discounts that."

"Sounds like you're discounting his perspective, too."

"I know, but—"

"Look, baby. I know it's hard. It's especially hard to wrap your mind around the fact that just because you found somebody who's perfect doesn't mean that everything about what they think and feel and do will be perfect. Relationships are about compromise. I think you should sit down and decide which is more important to you. Sticking to your guns or having Reece beside you."

"In other words, you're saying he wins."

Her mom laughed. "Since when did you revert to an eight-year-old? No, I'm not. I'm saying that you're the only one who can say. And maybe you've already made that decision. But the fact that we're having this conversation makes me think you're on the fence. So have a nice sit-down with yourself, and figure out which side of the fence you're going to climb down on."

"I love you, Mom," she said, because as painful as it might be to hear, everything her mom said was true. Especially when she considered that Reece was waiting for her on one side of the fence, his arms spread wide to hold her and keep her safe.

As soon as the call with her mom ended, Jenna dialed Reece, but he didn't answer. Jenna told herself that wasn't a bad omen, but when she tried three more times throughout the day and still got nothing, a sick feeling started to grow in her stomach. Had she waited too long? Had she screwed around and lost the best thing that ever happened to her?

"I need to go," she whispered to Brent, who looked at her like she'd grown two heads. "I need to find Reece."

"In case it escaped your notice, we're starting the contest in fifteen minutes."

She shifted her weight from foot to foot, feeling frantic. "But I have to tell him—"

"*Jenna.*" Brent's voice was harsh and no-nonsense.

She froze. "I'm losing it, aren't I?"

"Just a little. Come here." He pulled her into a hug. "Look, I know this thing with Reece is hard, but he's still going to be an asshole later tonight or tomorrow morning. Find him then," Brent continued, as Jenna giggled. "Right now, we have a contest about to start, the press in the audience, and a video crew from the local news ready to put together what we hope is one hell of a story. So get it together, okay? Because you need to enjoy this amazing event you organized."

"Right," she said. "I know."

But try as she might, she couldn't focus. Thank goodness she'd delegated. Everyone had a key job except her, as she'd planned to simply watch the audience. Fortunately, she'd asked a few others to do the same, because she was only hearing about half of what Beverly was saying on stage, and only noticing flashes of the buff, shirtless men who paraded up the red carpet and then across the stage.

Or, she was only half-paying attention until she heard Beverly say, "We have one last-minute contestant." Then Jenna started to stand, because what the hell? But Beverly kept talking, and Jenna had to sit again, because her knees were too weak to support her.

"A man who'd initially turned down an invitation to compete in the contest, but I know you all will be happy he changed his mind. Please welcome Reece Walker!"

The music started, and the crowd applauded as Reece strode down the red carpet, climbed the stairs to the stage, and pulled off his shirt—to the absolute delight of the women in the audience.

Reece smiled and flexed his muscles, but Jenna knew him well enough to know he was just going through the motions. What he was really doing was searching the crowd.

He was looking for her.

She wanted to wave. To stand. To do something. But she was too numb. She had no idea what he was doing up there, but she sat glued to her seat, desperate to find out.

"So I guess this is the part where I say something,"

Reece said. "And I should start by saying that I'm not actually up here to be a contestant. That's why I'm not on your ballot. But I have something to say to someone, and this was the best way I could think of to do it. And since I'm a manager here at The Fix, I have a little pull. So please, don't let my theatrics draw your attention away from our amazing contestants."

He cleared his throat and shifted his stance. To the audience, he probably looked cool and confident. But Jenna could see the nerves.

"I'm here tonight to apologize. To tell the woman I love that I screwed up. That I was so busy staying stuck in my ways and looking at the world through one boring lens, that I forgot to shift around and change my perspective."

He drew a breath. "The thing is, love is supposed to open us up, not close us off. I let my fears blot that out. I've been with the wrong woman so many times that I was scared to admit the right one was in my arms. And I was looking at other people and judging our relationship by them.

"I'm not saying it'll be easy," he continued. "It'll probably be hard at times. But I know it will be an adventure. Love always is, right? Anyway, I should have written this down, because I'm getting lost in my words. I'm not a speaker, and I don't particularly like being on stage. But I had to say this tonight, right now, because I couldn't wait any longer to tell her that I love her. Jenna Montgomery, I love you. I want you. More than that I need you. And even though I screwed up, I'm hoping that you will do me the very great honor of agreeing to be my wife."

She couldn't move. Her body was frozen to the chair, and tears were streaming down her cheeks. And when the spotlight found her—she was going to kill Taylor!—all she could do was nod like an idiot and soundlessly mouth, *I love you.*

Around her, the crowd burst into applause and Reece leaped off the stage, then hurried to her. He pulled her into his arms, cradling her as he continued toward the back of the bar, and the whole place was on its feet around her, laughing and applauding as Beverly, bless her, took control of the crowd.

He took her through the bar and then outside to the alley where he finally—*finally*—put her down and kissed her hard, the feel of him against her almost making her melt all over again.

"I can't live without you," he said when they came up for air. "I'm sorry I was a jerk."

"You weren't. I was. I don't want to force you to do something that makes you uncomfortable. I've been calling you all day to tell you that. I just want the two of us."

He pressed his hand to her belly. "Three."

"Yeah," she said, putting her hand over his. "Three."

They kissed again, long and lingering. "I mean it," she said, cupping his face because she had to keep touching him. Had to claim that connection. "I'm okay with not getting married. It's you I want, Reece. Only you."

"I know. I believe you. But you want a wedding, too. And I want to give it to you."

He dropped to one knee, then held out a small box. "I already asked on stage, but now I'm asking just you. Jenna Montgomery, will you marry me?"

"You bought me a ring?" It was a foolish question considering she'd opened the box to reveal a stunning diamond solitaire.

"It was my grandmother's. If you don't like it—"

"Are you kidding? It's amazing. I love it. And I love you."

The alley door burst open, interrupting one more kiss. "You two are the hottest thing on Twitter," Brent said, grinning ear to ear. "And the calendar contest is following a close second. All the phone lines are tied up with calls about when the next contest will be."

"That's great," Jenna said, her fingers twined with Reece's.

"Oh, and in case you're wondering. The vote's in. It was almost unanimous, so the count was easy." He looked up at Reece. "Congratulations, Mr. January. Apparently, your write-in vote swept the contest."

Reece's eyes went wide as Jenna and Brent laughed.

"This is your fault," Reece accused, aiming a mock glare at Jenna.

"Oh well," she said lightly. "I guess you can spank me later."

Brent burst out laughing, but from the look on Reece's face, that was very much on the agenda.

Jenna grinned, positively giddy, then held out her finger so he could slip on the ring. "And by the way, my answer is yes."

Epilogue

SPENCER DEAN LEANED against the wooden bar and sipped his bourbon while the crowd went crazy when the guy named Reece professed his love to a woman named Jenna.

Even he had to admit it was a sweet moment, and that was true even though he wasn't in a particularly sweet mood.

His eyes swept the bar, picking out the details as he mentally redesigned the place, adding features, moving walls, making it a showpiece.

In the process, his eyes found *her*. He hadn't realized she'd be here tonight, though he supposed he should have. She was just standing there, talking with the woman with the long ponytail who Spence had noticed doing behind the scenes work during the contest.

"Excuse me," he said, catching the attention of a waitress in a *The Fix on Sixth* T-shirt. "Would you tell that woman I'd like to talk to her. The blonde, not the brunette."

"Um, sure." Her brow furrowed, and he realized she

must think that he was trying to pick her up. "It's okay. I'm going to be working with her."

"Oh! You know Brooke, then."

"I know her all right." He shifted his stance, then worked to keep his voice even. "Brooke Hamlin's my ex-fiancée," he said.

And things were about to get interesting.

Hold On Tight Sneak Peek

Please enjoy this unedited peek at *Hold On Tight*!

CHAPTER ONE

"So that's it. That's my proposal." Brooke Hamlin forced herself not to wipe her sweaty palms on the gray silk blend of her designer skirt. Instead, she conjured her most winning smile and reminded herself to breathe.

"I understand that you only want six episodes for the first season," she continued. "But I really think that the goal should be to increase that in season two. Probably to eighteen episodes. And, although my working title is *The Business Plan*, I'm obviously open to change."

Shut up, Brooke, she told herself. *Shut up before you say something stupid and their eyes glaze over.*

The eyes in question belonged to two network executives, both with the kind of plastic Hollywood smiles that were totally unreadable. And seemed completely out of place in Austin, Texas, a town with a laid back vibe despite its recent growth.

"I just thought that since that's the title of my monthly

morning show segment that it made the most sense." *Why, why, why was she still talking?* "It's really quite popular," she added, and wondered if they'd notice if she took off one of her Christian Louboutin pumps and kicked her own ass.

She wasn't usually prone to nerves or chattiness, but she also wasn't usually in meetings that could literally change her life. Under the circumstances, maybe sweaty palms were a small price to pay.

Across the room, one of the executives—Molly—lifted her phone to her ear, reminding Brooke that a third exec in Los Angeles had seen and heard the entire pitch over a video call.

A moment later, Molly lowered her phone and indicated the colleague sitting beside her, a lanky guy whose name Brooke had forgotten.

"Brooke, we'd like to have a little pow-wow. If you could just wait here for a minute?"

"Oh. Sure."

Brooke watched them go, hoping that was a good sign. Then she moved to the window and put her forehead against the glass as she looked down the four stories from this suite in Austin's historic Driskill Hotel to the hustle-and-bustle of afternoon traffic on Sixth Street.

She'd always heard that The Driskill was haunted, but right now she disagreed. It wasn't haunted; it was magical. A place with the power to completely change her life. Or, more accurately, to justify her choices. To finally prove to her surgeon father and oncologist mother that she knew her own mind and could run her own life.

She'd dropped out of med school mid-way through her first semester because her dream had always been to fix property, not people. Growing up, she'd gravitated more toward her grandfather and uncle's property development business than to her parents' medical practices. A reality that they'd written off to a child playing with toys. They'd expected her to get serious about medicine and had paid for a top-notch education.

It hadn't been pretty when she'd thrown it all back in their faces. Her father's words, not hers. But she couldn't be a doctor when the interest just wasn't there. It wouldn't be fair to her. And it certainly wouldn't be fair to whatever patient happened to wander into her office.

Now, four years after walking away before her second semester at Southwestern Medical School, she'd finally launched The Business Plan, a commercial renovation company specializing in small businesses that are open to the public. Bars, restaurants, B&Bs, and the like. It was a hell of a lot of work, but she was in the black, if just barely, and her current focus was on getting more clients. Which meant she needed to be out there, front and center so that she was in the line of sight of people who might want to hire her.

To that end, she'd finagled a regular segment on one of Austin's local morning shows. In each segment, she featured her recent clients and explained to viewers how to tackle various property renovation projects, using video footage she shot during construction.

It wasn't going to win her an Emmy, but the station kept inviting her back, so she knew the ratings must be decent.

But if she could land *this* television show, then she'd finally, truly be on the map. She'd garner local press, interviews, the works. And the exposure would surely give her the clout and the contacts to tackle even more challenging projects.

And maybe—*maybe*—her father would stop looking at her like she was a failure.

Foolishly, she crossed her fingers. She tried to cross her

toes, too, but her spectacular shoes didn't allow for that, and she stumbled sideways as she tried to quickly put fingers and toes back in place when the door opened, and the two execs came back in, their bright smiles in place, but so generic that she couldn't tell if there was good news behind them.

"Have a seat, Brooke," Molly said, and this time when she smiled Brooke saw a dimple. *A genuine smile.* Her stomach flipped, and she hoped against hope that she wasn't reading the situation wrong.

Brooke did as she was told and perched on the edge of the sofa, her hands clasped on her knees so that she wouldn't fidget.

"As you know," the guy said, "we're on a tight schedule."

Brooke nodded. It had been less than a month ago that she'd seen the small announcement in the local paper. She'd learned that The Design and Destination Channel was accepting proposals for an Austin-based real estate show. She'd had less than a day to meet the deadline, and she'd thrown together a proposal, including video footage to prove she didn't look horrible on camera.

She'd been prepared to wait, but had heard back three days later. After an extensive phone interview, she'd received an invitation to this meeting. And the proposal she'd just presented wasn't much different from what had been on paper. Presumably, they just wanted to see if she was personable.

"We'll be honest," Molly added. "Andy and I both think that *The Business Plan* is the best proposal we have on the table."

Andy. That was his name.

Then Molly's words registered, and Brooke forced herself not to squeal. "That's great to hear." She managed not to keep her voice level, but from Molly's smile, Brooke knew that her excitement showed.

"We already have a crew in town and ready to go, and the plan is to get on the air soon with whichever show we end up choosing. As you know, we have a gap in our schedule that we're looking to fill with original content, and so this is going to be tight. But if all the pieces come together, it should work."

"Whatever you need me to do," Brooke said. "I'm ready to jump in."

Molly and Andy exchanged glances. "And the bar that you discussed in the proposal? The Fix on Sixth? They're ready to jump in, too?"

"The bar?" Brooke swallowed, thankful she hadn't taken off her light silk jacket, because she could feel her underarms getting sticky with nerves. "You're right that it would be perfect. But I thought I was clear that it was just one example of a possible location. I listed several in the proposal since we'd be focusing on a different location each episode."

Andy shook his head. "All property renovation programs do that. We want to go with a different spin. All episodes centered around the same location. In this case, we want to focus on the bar. The Fix on Sixth is perfect for what we have in mind."

"Oh. Oh, that's great." Brooke cleared her throat as she stood and returned to the window. She glanced down to Sixth Street, her gaze moving across the street and a few blocks to the east, so that she could see the bar in question.

Brooke's friend Amanda, a real estate broker, had told Brooke that The Fix needed a bit of a facelift to get it ready for a big marketing push, and that Brooke should apply for the job.

The way Amanda told it, The Fix had until the end of

the year to increase revenue. If they couldn't turn the place around and get it fully in the black, then the bar would close its doors, and Austin would lose a beloved venue. A place with great drinks, live music, and lots of local color.

Management was doing everything it could do keep the bar thriving, and that included sponsoring a Man of the Month calendar contest. The bar would hold live contests every couple of weeks, and by the fall, they'd have their twelve hot men to put on a calendar to sell to the public. If it worked as intended, the contest would draw in crowds— and the bar's management wanted to do a quick-and-dirty renovation to update the bar's look.

Brooke had figured that a stage full of hot guys would catch the network's eye, and so she'd included The Fix and a description of the calendar contest in the proposal. Apparently she'd been right, so she had to applaud her instincts. But she hadn't expected things to move quite so fast.

Because while *she* thought the plan was brilliant and that The Fix would undoubtedly want to be featured on a show, she hadn't actually pitched the idea to the bar. Yet.

That was supposed to happen tonight at her first meeting with Jenna Montgomery, the partner who was in charge of marketing. But surely Jenna would—

"Brooke?"

She looked up, then realized that she'd missed an entire thread of conversation.

"I'm sorry. I was looking at The Fix. I'm so excited I got lost in my thoughts." She swallowed, then offered a big Texas smile. "What did you say?"

"We want to confirm that The Fix's management is amenable to having a film crew there for the entire duration of their calendar contest."

"Oh! Yes, absolutely," she lied as she dried her palms

on her skirt. "The bar is one hundred percent all in." She cleared her throat, hoping that her nose wasn't growing. "In fact, I have a meeting there tonight. I'll tell them the good news."

"Wonderful." Molly's smile widened.

"So, um, what now? Do you have a contract I can forward my attorney?" Surely the folks at the bar would agree. Worst case, Brooke would bow out gracefully.

"Actually, there's one other thing we need to discuss first."

"Oh." Her smile was beginning to feel a little forced. She wanted to get out of that room so she could kick off her shoes and celebrate. Followed closely by an intense freak-out session and a few fervent prayers to the god of desperate women.

"We want you to partner with Spencer Dean."

Her throat tightened and her pulse skittered at the mention of the only man she'd ever loved. The man she'd planned to marry. To spend her life with.

The man who now despised her.

"Spencer?" She licked her lips. "I—I don't think he's working in television anymore."

For four of the last five years, Spencer and his partner Brian had starred in a house-flipping program. She'd watched only one episode. It hurt too much to see Spencer on screen. Those dark eyes that she'd once believed knew her so well. Those strong, calloused hands that had stroked her skin. His mustache and beard that had tickled her ear as he'd whispered sweet, sexy, decadent things.

He'd held her close and they'd made so many plans, so many promises. And then everything had shattered.

Brian. She fought a shudder of revulsion.

He was the other reason she hadn't watched Spencer's

show. It hurt to see Spence. But seeing Brian made her curl up into a useless ball of pain and self-loathing.

Their show had been called *Spencer's Place*, because it was as much about his personality as about the house-flipping. The show had been about to launch when the wedding plans had imploded, and it had run for four years before ending with a sudden and surprising finality. The tabloids speculated as to the reasons, but no one seemed to know for sure.

Neither did Brooke. But she knew Spencer well enough to know that if he'd decided it was time to back away from television, nothing would draw him back. Least of all her.

"It's true that he left *Spencer's Place*," Andy acknowledged, an edge to his voice. "But in doing so, he breached his contract. Spencer Dean still owes us one season of a television show. And we think this is the perfect vehicle."

"Oh, I don't know. I was envisioning this as a solo show." She realized she was holding the collar of her jacket closed and forced herself to relax.

"Brooke, darling." Molly's voice dripped with syrup. "You're beautiful, you're charming. You've got the poise and the good looks. What you aren't is a proven commodity. Spencer Dean is. Do you have any idea how popular he was during the course of the show?"

She did, of course. But she still couldn't imagine them wanting to put her on a show with Spencer. They might not know the details of their break-up, but they must know it wasn't pretty.

But then the real truth hit her. It wasn't her proposal that intrigued them. It wasn't even the renovations or the sexy men at The Fix. Not entirely, anyway.

What the producers wanted was drama. And as soon as they saw her name on a proposal, they saw a way to manufacture chaos. This was reality TV, after all. And even for a property renovation program, the network was going to want fireworks.

She shot a hard look at both Molly and Andy. "Really," she said firmly. "That's not at all what I had in mind."

"Let me be more clear." The syrup in Molly's voice had turned to steel. "The network wants you and Spencer. Without Spencer Dean, there is no show."

Who's Your Man of the Month?

When a group of fiercely determined friends realize their beloved hang-out is in danger of closing, they take matters into their own hands to bring back customers lost to a competing bar. Fighting fire with a heat of their own, they double down with the broad shoulders, six-pack abs, and bare chests of dozens of hot, local guys who they cajole, prod, and coerce into auditioning for a Man of the Month calendar.

But it's not just the fate of the bar that's at stake. Because as things heat up, each of the men meets his match in this sexy, flirty, and compelling binge-read romance series of twelve novels releasing every other week from *New York Times* bestselling author J. Kenner.

"With each novel featuring a favorite romance trope— beauty and the beast, billionaire bad boys, friends to lovers, second chance romance, secret baby, and more—[the Man of the Month] series hits the heart and soul of romance." *New York Times* bestselling author Carly Phillips

Down On Me
Hold On Tight
Need You Now
Start Me Up
Get It On
In Your Eyes
Turn Me On
Shake It Up
All Night Long
In Too Deep
Light My Fire
Walk The Line

and don't miss Bar Bites: A Man of the Month Cookbook!

Meet Damien Stark

Only his passion could set her free…

Release Me
Claim Me
Complete Me
Anchor Me
Lost With Me

The Stark Saga by J. Kenner

Meet Damien Stark in Release Me, *book 1 of the wildly sensual series that's left millions of readers breathless …*

Chapter One

A cool ocean breeze caresses my bare shoulders, and I shiver, wishing I'd taken my roommate's advice and brought a shawl with me tonight. I arrived in Los Angeles only four days ago, and I haven't yet adjusted to the concept of summer temperatures changing with the setting of the sun. In Dallas, June is hot, July is hotter, and August is hell.

Not so in California, at least not by the beach. LA Lesson Number One: Always carry a sweater if you'll be out after dark.

Of course, I could leave the balcony and go back inside to the party. Mingle with the millionaires. Chat up the celebrities. Gaze dutifully at the paintings. It is a gala art opening, after all, and my boss brought me here to meet and greet and charm and chat. Not to lust over the panorama that is coming alive in front of me. Bloodred clouds bursting against the pale orange sky. Blue-gray waves shimmering with dappled gold.

I press my hands against the balcony rail and lean forward, drawn to the intense, unreachable beauty of the setting sun. I regret that I didn't bring the battered Nikon I've had since high school. Not that it would have fit in my itty-bitty beaded purse. And a bulky camera bag paired with a little black dress is a big, fat fashion no-no.

But this is my very first Pacific Ocean sunset, and I'm determined to document the moment. I pull out my iPhone and snap a picture.

"Almost makes the paintings inside seem redundant, doesn't it?" I recognize the throaty, feminine voice and turn to face Evelyn Dodge, retired actress turned agent turned patron of the arts—and my hostess for the evening.

"I'm so sorry. I know I must look like a giddy tourist, but we don't have sunsets like this in Dallas."

"Don't apologize," she says. "I pay for that view every month when I write the mortgage check. It damn well better be spectacular."

I laugh, immediately more at ease.

"Hiding out?"

"Excuse me?"

"You're Carl's new assistant, right?" she asks, referring to my boss of three days.

"Nikki Fairchild."

"I remember now. Nikki from Texas." She looks me up and down, and I wonder if she's disappointed that I don't have big hair and cowboy boots. "So who does he want you to charm?"

"Charm?" I repeat, as if I don't know exactly what she means.

She cocks a single brow. "Honey, the man would rather walk on burning coals than come to an art show. He's fishing for investors and you're the bait." She makes a rough noise in the back of her throat. "Don't worry. I won't press you to tell me who. And I don't blame you for hiding out. Carl's brilliant, but he's a bit of a prick."

"It's the brilliant part I signed on for," I say, and she barks out a laugh.

The truth is that she's right about me being the bait. "Wear a cocktail dress," Carl had said. "Something flirty."

Seriously? I mean, *Seriously?*

I should have told him to wear his own damn cocktail dress. But I didn't. Because I want this job. I fought to get this job. Carl's company, C-Squared Technologies, successfully launched three web-based products in the last eighteen months. That track record had caught the industry's eye, and Carl had been hailed as a man to watch.

More important from my perspective, that meant he was a man to learn from, and I'd prepared for the job interview with an intensity bordering on obsession. Landing the position had been a huge coup for me. So what if he wanted me to wear something flirty? It was a small price to pay.

Shit.

"I need to get back to being the bait," I say.

"Oh, hell. Now I've gone and made you feel either guilty or self-conscious. Don't be. Let them get liquored up in there first. You catch more flies with alcohol anyway. Trust me. I know."

She's holding a pack of cigarettes, and now she taps one out, then extends the pack to me. I shake my head. I love the smell of tobacco—it reminds me of my grandfather—but actually inhaling the smoke does nothing for me.

"I'm too old and set in my ways to quit," she says. "But God forbid I smoke in my own damn house. I swear, the mob would burn me in effigy. You're not going to start lecturing me on the dangers of secondhand smoke, are you?"

"No," I promise.

"Then how about a light?"

I hold up the itty-bitty purse. "One lipstick, a credit card, my driver's license, and my phone."

"No condom?"

"I didn't think it was that kind of party," I say dryly.

"I knew I liked you." She glances around the balcony. "What the hell kind of party am I throwing if I don't even have one goddamn candle on one goddamn table? Well, fuck it." She puts the unlit cigarette to her mouth and inhales, her eyes closed and her expression rapturous. I can't help but like her. She wears hardly any makeup, in stark contrast to all the other women here tonight, myself included, and her dress is more of a caftan, the batik pattern as interesting as the woman herself.

She's what my mother would call a brassy broad— loud, large, opinionated, and self-confident. My mother would hate her. I think she's awesome.

She drops the unlit cigarette onto the tile and grinds it

with the toe of her shoe. Then she signals to one of the catering staff, a girl dressed all in black and carrying a tray of champagne glasses.

The girl fumbles for a minute with the sliding door that opens onto the balcony, and I imagine those flutes tumbling off, breaking against the hard tile, the scattered shards glittering like a wash of diamonds.

I picture myself bending to snatch up a broken stem. I see the raw edge cutting into the soft flesh at the base of my thumb as I squeeze. I watch myself clutching it tighter, drawing strength from the pain, the way some people might try to extract luck from a rabbit's foot.

The fantasy blurs with memory, jarring me with its potency. It's fast and powerful, and a little disturbing because I haven't needed the pain in a long time, and I don't understand why I'm thinking about it now, when I feel steady and in control.

I am fine, I think. *I am fine, I am fine, I am fine.*

"Take one, honey," Evelyn says easily, holding a flute out to me.

I hesitate, searching her face for signs that my mask has slipped and she's caught a glimpse of my rawness. But her face is clear and genial.

"No, don't you argue," she adds, misinterpreting my hesitation. "I bought a dozen cases and I hate to see good alcohol go to waste. Hell no," she adds when the girl tries to hand her a flute. "I hate the stuff. Get me a vodka. Straight up. Chilled. Four olives. Hurry up, now. Do you want me to dry up like a leaf and float away?"

The girl shakes her head, looking a bit like a twitchy, frightened rabbit. Possibly one that had sacrificed his foot for someone else's good luck.

Evelyn's attention returns to me. "So how do you like LA? What have you seen? Where have you been? Have you bought a map of the stars yet? Dear God, tell me you're not getting sucked into all that tourist bullshit."

"Mostly I've seen miles of freeway and the inside of my apartment."

"Well, that's just sad. Makes me even more glad that Carl dragged your skinny ass all the way out here tonight."

I've put on fifteen welcome pounds since the years when my mother monitored every tiny thing that went in my mouth, and while I'm perfectly happy with my size-eight ass, I wouldn't describe it as skinny. I know Evelyn means it as a compliment, though, and so I smile. "I'm glad he brought me, too. The paintings really are amazing."

"Now don't do that—don't you go sliding into the polite-conversation routine. No, no," she says before I can protest. "I'm sure you mean it. Hell, the paintings are wonderful. But you're getting the flat-eyed look of a girl on her best behavior, and we can't have that. Not when I was getting to know the real you."

"Sorry," I say. "I swear I'm not fading away on you."

Because I genuinely like her, I don't tell her that she's wrong—she hasn't met the real Nikki Fairchild. She's met Social Nikki who, much like Malibu Barbie, comes with a complete set of accessories. In my case, it's not a bikini and a convertible. Instead, I have the *Elizabeth Fairchild Guide for Social Gatherings*.

My mother's big on rules. She claims it's her Southern upbringing. In my weaker moments, I agree. Mostly, I just think she's a controlling bitch. Since the first time she took me for tea at the Mansion at Turtle Creek in Dallas at age three, I have had the rules drilled into my head. How to walk, how to talk, how to dress. What to eat, how much to drink, what kinds of jokes to tell.

I have it all down, every trick, every nuance, and I wear

my practiced pageant smile like armor against the world. The result being that I don't think I could truly be myself at a party even if my life depended on it.

This, however, is not something Evelyn needs to know.

"Where exactly are you living?" she asks.

"Studio City. I'm sharing a condo with my best friend from high school."

"Straight down the 101 for work and then back home again. No wonder you've only seen concrete. Didn't anyone tell you that you should have taken an apartment on the Westside?"

"Too pricey to go it alone," I admit, and I can tell that my admission surprises her. When I make the effort—like when I'm Social Nikki—I can't help but look like I come from money. Probably because I do. Come from it, that is. But that doesn't mean I brought it with me.

"How old are you?"

"Twenty-four."

Evelyn nods sagely, as if my age reveals some secret about me. "You'll be wanting a place of your own soon enough. You call me when you do and we'll find you someplace with a view. Not as good as this one, of course, but we can manage something better than a freeway on-ramp."

"It's not that bad, I promise."

"Of course it's not," she says in a tone that says the exact opposite. "As for views," she continues, gesturing toward the now-dark ocean and the sky that's starting to bloom with stars, "you're welcome to come back anytime and share mine."

"I might take you up on that," I admit. "I'd love to bring a decent camera back here and take a shot or two."

"It's an open invitation. I'll provide the wine and you can provide the entertainment. A young woman loose in the city. Will it be a drama? A rom-com? Not a tragedy, I hope. I love a good cry as much as the next woman, but I like you. You need a happy ending."

I tense, but Evelyn doesn't know she's hit a nerve. That's why I moved to LA, after all. New life. New story. New Nikki.

I ramp up the Social Nikki smile and lift my champagne flute. "To happy endings. And to this amazing party. I think I've kept you from it long enough."

"Bullshit," she says. "I'm the one monopolizing you, and we both know it."

We slip back inside, the buzz of alcohol-fueled conversation replacing the soft calm of the ocean.

"The truth is, I'm a terrible hostess. I do what I want, talk to whoever I want, and if my guests feel slighted they can damn well deal with it."

I gape. I can almost hear my mother's cries of horror all the way from Dallas.

"Besides," she continues, "this party isn't supposed to be about me. I put together this little shindig to introduce Blaine and his art to the community. He's the one who should be doing the mingling, not me. I may be fucking him, but I'm not going to baby him."

Evelyn has completely destroyed my image of how a hostess for the not-to-be-missed social event of the weekend is supposed to behave, and I think I'm a little in love with her for that.

"I haven't met Blaine yet. That's him, right?" I point to a tall reed of a man. He is bald, but sports a red goatee. I'm pretty sure it's not his natural color. A small crowd hums around him, like bees drawing nectar from a flower. His outfit is certainly as bright as one.

"That's my little center of attention, all right," Evelyn says. "The man of the hour. Talented, isn't he?" Her hand sweeps out to indicate her massive living room. Every wall is covered with paintings. Except for a few benches, whatever furniture was once in the room has been removed and replaced with easels on which more paintings stand.

I suppose technically they are portraits. The models are nudes, but these aren't like anything you would see in a classical art book. There's something edgy about them. Something provocative and raw. I can tell that they are expertly conceived and carried out, and yet they disturb me, as if they reveal more about the person viewing the portrait than about the painter or the model.

As far as I can tell, I'm the only one with that reaction. Certainly the crowd around Blaine is glowing. I can hear the gushing praise from here.

"I picked a winner with that one," Evelyn says. "But let's see. Who do you want to meet? Rip Carrington and Lyle Tarpin? Those two are guaranteed drama, that's for damn sure, and your roommate will be jealous as hell if you chat them up."

"She will?"

Evelyn's brows arch up. "Rip and Lyle? They've been feuding for weeks." She narrows her eyes at me. "The fiasco about the new season of their sitcom? It's all over the Internet? You really don't know them?"

"Sorry," I say, feeling the need to apologize. "My school schedule was pretty intense. And I'm sure you can imagine what working for Carl is like."

Speaking of ...

I glance around, but I don't see my boss anywhere.

"That is one serious gap in your education," Evelyn says. "Culture—and yes, pop culture counts—is just as important as—what did you say you studied?"

"I don't think I mentioned it. But I have a double major in electrical engineering and computer science."

"So you've got brains and beauty. See? That's something else we have in common. Gotta say, though, with an education like that, I don't see why you signed up to be Carl's secretary."

I laugh. "I'm not, I swear. Carl was looking for someone with tech experience to work with him on the business side of things, and I was looking for a job where I could learn the business side. Get my feet wet. I think he was a little hesitant to hire me at first—my skills definitely lean toward tech—but I convinced him I'm a fast learner."

She peers at me. "I smell ambition."

I lift a shoulder in a casual shrug. "It's Los Angeles. Isn't that what this town is all about?"

"Ha! Carl's lucky he's got you. It'll be interesting to see how long he keeps you. But let's see … who here would intrigue you …?"

She casts about the room, finally pointing to a fifty-something man holding court in a corner. "That's Charles Maynard," she says. "I've known Charlie for years. Intimidating as hell until you get to know him. But it's worth it. His clients are either celebrities with name recognition or power brokers with more money than God. Either way, he's got all the best stories."

"He's a lawyer?"

"With Bender, Twain & McGuire. Very prestigious firm."

"I know," I say, happy to show that I'm not entirely ignorant, despite not knowing Rip or Lyle. "One of my closest friends works for the firm. He started here but he's in their New York office now."

"Well, come on, then, Texas. I'll introduce you." We take one step in that direction, but then Evelyn stops me. Maynard has pulled out his phone, and is shouting instructions at someone. I catch a few well-placed curses and eye

Evelyn sideways. She looks unconcerned "He's a pussycat at heart. Trust me, I've worked with him before. Back in my agenting days, we put together more celebrity biopic deals for our clients than I can count. And we fought to keep a few tell-alls off the screen, too." She shakes her head, as if reliving those glory days, then pats my arm. "Still, we'll wait 'til he calms down a bit. In the meantime, though …"

She trails off, and the corners of her mouth turn down in a frown as she scans the room again. "I don't think he's here yet, but—oh! Yes! Now *there's* someone you should meet. And if you want to talk views, the house he's building has one that makes my view look like, well, like yours." She points toward the entrance hall, but all I see are bobbing heads and haute couture. "He hardly ever accepts invitations, but we go way back," she says.

I still can't see who she's talking about, but then the crowd parts and I see the man in profile. Goose bumps rise on my arms, but I'm not cold. In fact, I'm suddenly very, very warm.

He's tall and so handsome that the word is almost an insult. But it's more than that. It's not his looks, it's his *presence*. He commands the room simply by being in it, and I realize that Evelyn and I aren't the only ones looking at him. The entire crowd has noticed his arrival. He must feel the weight of all those eyes, and yet the attention doesn't faze him at all. He smiles at the girl with the champagne, takes a glass, and begins to chat casually with a woman who approaches him, a simpering smile stretched across her face.

"Damn that girl," Evelyn says. "She never did bring me my vodka."

But I barely hear her. "Damien Stark," I say. My voice surprises me. It's little more than breath.

Evelyn's brows rise so high I notice the movement in my peripheral vision. "Well, how about that?" she says knowingly. "Looks like I guessed right."

"You did," I admit. "Mr. Stark is just the man I want to see."

I hope you enjoyed the excerpt! Grab your own copy of Release Me ... or any of the books in the series now!

The Original Trilogy
Release Me
Claim Me
Complete Me

And Beyond...
Anchor Me
Lost With Me

"J. Kenner never disappoints~her books just get better and better." - *Mom's Guilty Pleasure (on Wicked Grind)*

"I don't think J. Kenner could write a bad story if she tried. … Wicked Grind is a great beginning to what I'm positive will be a very successful series. … The line forms here." *iScream Books (On Wicked Grind)*

"Scorching, sweet, and soul-searing, *Anchor Me* is the ultimate love story that stands the test of time and tribulation. THE TRUEST LOVE!" *Bookalicious Babes Blog (on Anchor Me)*

"J. Kenner has brought this couple to life and the character connection that I have to these two holds no bounds and that is testament to J. Kenner's writing ability." *The Romance Cover (on Anchor Me)*

"J. Kenner writes an emotional and personal story line. … The premise will captivate your imagination; the characters will break your heart; the romance continues to push the envelope." *The Reading Café (on Anchor Me)*

"Kenner may very well have cornered the market on sinfully attractive, dominant antiheroes and the women who swoon for them . . ." *Romantic Times*

"*Wanted* is another J. Kenner masterpiece . . . This was an intriguing look at self-discovery and forbidden love all wrapped into a neat little action-suspense package. There was plenty of sexual tension and eventually action. Evan was hot, hot, hot! Together, they were combustible. But can we expect anything less from J. Kenner?" *Reading Haven*

"*Wanted* by J. Kenner is the whole package! A toe-curling smokin' hot read, full of incredible characters and a brilliant storyline that you won't be able to get enough of. I can't wait for the next book in this series . . . I'm hooked!" *Flirty & Dirty Book Blog*

"J. Kenner's evocative writing thrillingly captures the power of physical attraction, the pull of longing, the universe-altering effect one person can have on another. . . . *Claim Me* has the emotional depth to back up the sex . . . Every scene is infused with both erotic tension, and the tension of wondering what lies beneath Damien's veneer – and how and when it will be revealed." *Heroes and Heartbreakers*

"*Claim Me* by J. Kenner is an erotic, sexy and exciting ride. The story between Damien and Nikki is amazing and written beautifully. The intimate and detailed sex scenes will leave you fanning yourself to cool down. With the writing style of Ms. Kenner you almost feel like you are there in the story riding along the emotional rollercoaster with Damien and Nikki." *Fresh Fiction*

"PERFECT for fans of *Fifty Shades of Grey* and *Bared to You.* *Release Me* is a powerful and erotic romance novel that is sure to make adult romance readers sweat, sigh and swoon." *Reading, Eating & Dreaming Blog*

"I will admit, I am in the 'I loved *Fifty Shades*' camp, but after reading *Release Me*, Mr. Grey only scratches the surface compared to Damien Stark." *Cocktails and Books Blog*

"It is not often when a book is so amazingly well-written that I find it hard to even begin to accurately describe it . . . I recommend this book to everyone who is interested in a passionate love story." *Romancebookworm's Reviews*

"The story is one that will rank up with the *Fifty Shades* and Cross Fire trilogies." *Incubus Publishing Blog*

"The plot is complex, the characters engaging, and J. Kenner's passionate writing brings it all perfectly together." *Harlequin Junkie*

Also by J. Kenner

The Stark Saga Novels:

Only his passion could set her free…

Meet Damien Stark

The Original Trilogy

Release Me

Claim Me

Complete Me

And Beyond…

Anchor Me

Lost With Me

Stark Ever After

(Stark Saga novellas):

Happily ever after is just the beginning.

The passion between Damien & Nikki continues.

Take Me

Have Me

Play My Game

Seduce Me

Unwrap Me

Deepest Kiss

Entice Me

Hold Me

Please Me

The Steele Books/Stark International:

He was the only man who made her feel alive.

Say My Name

On My Knees

Under My Skin

Take My Dare (includes short story Steal My Heart)

Stark International Novellas:

Meet Jamie & Ryan-so hot it sizzles.

Tame Me

Tempt Me

S.I.N. Trilogy:

It was wrong for them to be together...

...but harder to stay apart.

Dirtiest Secret

Hottest Mess

Sweetest Taboo

Stand alone novels:

Most Wanted:

Three powerful, dangerous men.

Three sensual, seductive women.

Wanted

Heated

Ignited

Wicked Nights (Stark World):

Sometimes it feels so damn good to be bad.

Wicked Grind

Wicked Dirty

Wicked Torture

Man of the Month

Who's your man of the month …?

Down On Me

Hold On Tight

Need You Now

Start Me Up

Get It On

In Your Eyes

Turn Me On

Shake It Up

All Night Long

In Too Deep

Light My Fire

Walk The Line

Bar Bites: A Man of the Month Cookbook(by J. Kenner &
Suzanne M. Johnson)

Additional Titles

Wild Thing

One Night (A Stark World short story in the Second Chances anthology)

Also by Julie Kenner

229

Also by Julie Kenner

Caress of Darkness
Find Me In Darkness
Find Me In Pleasure
Find Me In Passion
Caress of Pleasure

The Blood Lily Chronicles:
Tainted
Torn
Turned

Rising Storm:
Rising Storm: Tempest Rising
Rising Storm: Quiet Storm

Devil May Care:
Seducing Sin
Tempting Fate

About the Author

J. Kenner (aka Julie Kenner) is the *New York Times*, *USA Today*, *Publishers Weekly*, *Wall Street Journal* and #1 International bestselling author of over eighty novels, novellas and short stories in a variety of genres.

JK has been praised by *Publishers Weekly* as an author with a "flair for dialogue and eccentric characterizations" and by *RT Bookclub* for having "cornered the market on sinfully attractive, dominant antiheroes and the women who swoon for them." A five-time finalist for Romance Writers of America's prestigious RITA award, JK took home the first RITA trophy awarded in the category of erotic romance in 2014 for her novel, *Claim Me* (book 2 of her Stark Trilogy).

In her previous career as an attorney, JK worked as a lawyer in Southern California and Texas. She currently lives in Central Texas, with her husband, two daughters, and two rather spastic cats.

Text JKenner to 21000 to subscribe to JK's text alerts.

Visit www.jkenner.com for more ways to stay in the know!

87471150R00134

Made in the USA
Columbia, SC
14 January 2018